The Apostrophe Thief
You Have the Right to Remain Silent
In-Laws and Outlaws
Good King Sauerkraut
He Huffed and He Puffed
But He Was Already Dead When I Got There
Kill Fee
The Renewable Virgin
The Three-Minute Universe
A Chorus of Detectives
Prima Donna at Large
A Cadenza for Caruso
Your Eyelids Are Growing Heavy
First Gravedigger
Liars and Tyrants and People Who Turn Blue
The Fourth Wall
Under the Canopy
Bibblings
Pillars of Salt
An Exercise for Madmen

FARE PLAY

A Mystery with Marian Larch

Barbara Paul

SCRIBNER

New York   London   Toronto   Sydney   Tokyo   Singapore

SCRIBNER
Simon & Schuster Inc.
1230 Avenue of the Americas
New York, NY 10020

SCRIBNER and design are registered trademarks of Simon & Schuster Inc.
Manufactured in the United States of America

1   3   5   7   9   10   8   6   4   2

Library of Congress Cataloging-in-Publication Data
Paul, Barbara, 1931–
Fare play: a mystery with Marian Larch/Barbara Paul.
p. cm.
1. Larch, Marian (Fictitious character)—Fiction. 2. Policewomen—
New York (N.Y.)—Fiction. I. Title.
PS3566.A82615F3   1995   94–34640   CIP
813'.54—dc20

ISBN 0-684-19715-4

FARE PLAY

* 1 *

He was looking at a fortyish woman carrying a cheap all-weather coat over her arm and wearing a black-and-white polka-dot dress. Square neck, oversized shoulder pads, voluminous knee-length skirt . . . the sort of thing his mother wore back in the fifties. This woman had what was once a good haircut; but she'd let it go too long between trims and now looked on the verge of messy. Campy and messy. Didn't the woman own a mirror?

Was she the one he was here to meet? He hoped not. All Virgil had said was to carry a copy of *Opera News* prominently displayed and the courier would find him. He'd left the magazine lying out in the open on the small table in The Token Bar; now he signaled to the waiter. One more martini and he'd leave. He didn't like waiting for women.

Not that it had to be a woman; but Virgil typically did use women as couriers. Artistic types trying to make ends meet, girl graduates learning their brand-new degrees from Columbia weren't worth spit, mothers unable to take on full-time jobs. All Virgil demanded of them was that they be on time, do exactly as they were told, and ask no questions. For this they were paid promptly and in cash. What the IRS didn't know wouldn't hurt it.

The door of the bar opened and a young woman came in,

alone, shrugging out of her coat immediately. The waiting man smiled in approval: short skirt, high heels, careful make-up, well-tended hair. But he knew this one wouldn't be Virgil's courier; too expensive, for one thing. For another: too noticeable.

"*Opera News*." The woman in the polka-dot dress slid into the chair opposite his.

"You're late," he said coldly.

"I didn't spot you right off." She glanced at the magazine lying on the table. "I thought you'd be holding it. Reading it, like."

The man didn't answer. He held out his hand.

The polka-dot woman opened a purse the size of a saddlebag and extracted a large mailing envelope which she handed over. The seal on the back was intact. She didn't get up and leave, as she was supposed to, but instead sat waiting expectantly.

"Was there something else?" he asked shortly.

A look of mild disappointment crept into her eyes. She shook her head and stood up. He watched her go with barely concealed contempt. Damned if he'd buy a drink for that frump.

He broke the seal on the envelope. Inside were two five-by-seven glossies and a personal data sheet. Anthony Pasquellini, greengrocer, Mulberry Street. Someone was willing to pay Virgil's exorbitant fee to get rid of an Italian vegetable-seller? This Pasquellini couldn't be connected; the Mafia took care of its own problems. The man wasted no mental energy wondering about it; he never wondered about it.

He finished his martini and put on his overcoat. Outside, perhaps two hours of daylight left; the markets in Little Italy would still be open. If the crowds were big and noisy, he could take care of this one before dinner.

He hailed a cab and went to work.

*   *   *

The woman had to make an effort not to slump as she sat on the bus. She'd collect her fee and go home; maybe she'd have some time to herself before Hank got there and started making his demands. She just didn't feel like playing the admiring audience today. Today? Today, yesterday, the day before . . . she was tired of Hank, tired of the role he'd cast her in, tired of listening to him brag about whatever deal-of-a-lifetime he was at that very moment putting together. She was tired of never having enough money. She was in a rut and didn't see how to get out.

Knowing that, she'd worn her new black-and-white polka-dot dress to make herself feel better. It didn't work. And then to top things off, that cold-eyed bastard in The Token Bar wouldn't even buy her a drink.

He was a new one—new to her, at any rate. She didn't like the kind of people Virgil was sending her to meet lately; they were hard and dangerous-looking, men who made it impossible for her to go on pretending that Virgil was just an ordinary businessman doing nothing more than a little shady wheeling and dealing on the side. The men Virgil was sending her to meet made her uneasy, and she didn't know what to do about it. Virgil was not interested in employee complaints. But he paid in cash and he never wrote her name on any tax form. Still, it was just one more rut she was stuck in.

Virgil's man was waiting for her outside Cinema I on Third Avenue. Today he was wearing the long mustard-colored coat that made him look even more sallow than he already was. He handed her the familiar small brown envelope and turned away without a word. In the nearly thirty times she'd kept an appointment with the paymaster, he'd uttered only one word and that was the first time they'd met. He'd said:

"Identification?" When she'd showed him her ID, he'd handed her her first envelope and established the routine they'd been following ever since.

No talk. No personal contact. Ever.

The polka-dot woman was out of his mind even before she was out of his sight. The sallow-faced man had one more pay-off to make, and he was a bit worried about it. Grad student at NYU, always late. Unreliable, in the paymaster's opinion. But Virgil picked them, he didn't. And Virgil didn't welcome suggestions.

They were to meet in a pizza parlor on West Fourth. The paymaster took the subway, pocketing the difference between that and cab fare from the transportation allowance Virgil gave him. If *he* had been running the show, he'd do away with the couriers altogether; but Virgil wanted a buffer of people between his paymaster and the Talent. Careful man, Virgil.

She wasn't in the pizza parlor. Swearing to himself, the paymaster ordered a cut and a Coke and settled down to wait. He stretched a second cut out as long as he could and then went outside to wait there, turning up the collar of his mustard-colored coat against the February wind. When his watch told him she was forty minutes late, he left. This time he took a cab back uptown.

The sign on the office door said TWENTY-FIRST CENTURY CONSULTANTS; and underneath in smaller letters, WE PLAN FOR THE FUTURE. The office was deliberately nondescript, like thousands of other small offices scattered across Manhattan similarly doing business of a vaguely designated nature. The only person the paymaster had ever seen there was a woman who sat in the front office; the door to the back office was always closed. The paymaster had never met Virgil.

"My last contact didn't show," he said abruptly. "I told you that girl was unreliable."

The receptionist frowned. "How long did you wait?"

"An hour. I don't even know if she met with the Talent or not."

She opened a drawer of her desk. "Leave the pay packet with me. I'll give you a receipt."

The paymaster jerked his head toward the closed office door. "I'd better talk to Virgil."

"He didn't come in today." She wrote out the receipt.

That made the third time he'd asked to speak to the boss and been told he wasn't there. If he could be trusted to handle Virgil's money, then he sure as hell could be trusted to know what the boss looked like. Irritated, he stepped over to the closed door and threw it open—to find another nondescript office. Empty.

"I *said* he didn't come in today!" the receptionist spoke sharply. "Here's your receipt."

Defeated, the paymaster turned over his uncollected brown envelope. "Can I make an appointment to see him?"

"I'll ask," she said noncommittally.

Sure, you will, he thought sourly, and left.

She waited until she heard the elevator doors open and close; even then she looked out into the hall to make sure the man in the atrocious mustard coat had really gone. Then she went back into the office and locked the door. She powered up the computer and waited while the communications program loaded automatically. The only number in the dialing directory was hidden from her; she pressed the code number 1 and waited.

Two messages to pass on to Virgil today: *Contact 4 no show* and *Paymaster B wants a meet*. Usually she had to wait a day for a reply, but this time the answer came immediately: *No follow-through*. And that, she'd learned, meant Virgil would take care of the problem(s) himself and she was to forget about it.

She'd love to forget about it. She'd love to forget this damned office and what happened here. What the paymaster didn't know was that she had no more idea of who Virgil was than he did. But whoever he was, he was nothing more than a filthy murderer—and she was his unwilling accomplice.

It was the Social Security number that was holding her here. The lack of a new number for a false name forced her to stay in the job she'd been blackmailed into taking. How this, this *Virgil* had found out what she'd done . . . no one could have found out! But Virgil had, damn him, and he'd coerced her into coming in here and doing *servant* work for him . . . she could almost understand hiring a killer, when she thought of Virgil. No; don't dwell on that.

Think about getting out. All her spare time had been spent visiting outlying graveyards until finally she'd found what she was looking for in Greenwood Cemetery in Brooklyn: the grave of a woman born only the year before she was but who'd been dead for eleven years. Using the dead woman's name, she'd rented an unfurnished studio apartment to give herself a mailing address. Then she'd gotten a driver's license under her new name; and with this form of legitimate ID in hand, she'd gone into the Social Security office claiming she'd lost her card and applied for a replacement. And as soon as the card came . . . the scheme might work, might not. But it was the only way she could think of that would let her leave New York, find a new town, a new job. A new start.

Any day now that envelope would come, the one from the Social Security office with her new name and number. And then she'd be gone. Everything else was ready.

And when that monster Virgil goes down, I won't be here to go with him. The thought gave her immense satisfaction—not only the thought of her own escape, but the thought that Virgil would, eventually, be caught. He had to be. In spite of all his precautions, in spite of the careful chain of command he'd built, Virgil just had too many people working for him for some weak link not to be in there somewhere. Her main regret was that she would not be here to watch it happen. But someday, some cop would figure out what was going on, and that was the day Virgil's murder-for-hire business would start unraveling.

Some day. Some cop.

* 2 *

Lieutenant Marian Larch picked up a report from the pile on the desk before her. An early-morning fire in the Lord & Taylor stockroom had resulted in no deaths or injuries. Good, for more than the obvious reason; none of her detectives would be needed to investigate. She finished the report and started to put it aside. But something teased at her, half-caught her attention; she went back and read it again. What was odd, what was different about this report?

Aha. No misspellings.

Wonder of wonders—a cop who could spell. The first officer on the scene of the fire, and the writer of the report, was a bluesuit named Strauss. Marian concentrated, but she couldn't summon up a face to match the name. So many new faces, and not yet time enough to learn them all. Well, that would come.

She read the rest of the reports on her desk. Nothing major; Captain Murtaugh would be happy. *Marian* was happy. Home at a decent hour: she thought she remembered what that was like. She gathered up the reports and took them to the captain's office.

"What?" Murtaugh barked.

Marian ignored his end-of-the-day gruffness and told him what. "Last night's attempted break-in at Liebowitz Jewelry turned out to be a false alarm—literally. A rat gnawing through the insulation of a wire set off the electronics. Officer on the scene told Liebowitz to call an exterminator instead of a security expert."

Murtaugh grunted. "What next?"

"The fire in the stockroom at Lord and Taylor—nobody hurt. Bomb and Arson gets this one."

"Cause?"

"First officer thought he smelled gasoline."

The captain nodded. "Not our problem."

Marian cleared her throat. "The only thing new I have on the steroids smuggling—"

"Pass it on to the Two-three. They're claiming jurisdiction and we're going to let them have it."

She made a note: 23rd Precinct. "Next, two kitchen workers at Riccardo's Ristorante on East Thirty-sixth went at each other with butcher knives," she said. "Both men were treated for superficial cuts and taken downtown to the holding cells. Walker and Dowd are at the restaurant now, interviewing witnesses."

Murtaugh waved a hand dismissively; just another knife fight. "Anything else?"

Marian had saved the best for last. "You'll be happy to hear," she said with a smile, "that our friend Dmitri is at last in custody. Perlmutter just called it in."

Murtaugh snorted. "About time. How'd he get him?"

"Luck. Perlmutter was standing on the street talking to a bluesuit when some guy ran up yelling that Dmitri was 'signing' the Statler right then. They caught him in the act."

"In broad daylight? The guy either has a screw loose or he wanted to be caught." Dmitri was the nom-de-spray-paint of a mysterious "artist" who had taken it on himself to decorate a number of Manhattan's edifices with curious abstract designs. It was only when you looked closely that you could see the letters forming the word "Dmitri" worked into each design. Having a Dmitri signature on the building had become a camp status symbol in some quarters; but the *Times* had printed a no-nonsense article contending that defacing a beautiful building was still vandalism and would never be art. "Is it a kid?" Murtaugh asked.

"No, Perlmutter says he's in his late thirties," Marian replied. "Postal worker from Queens, quiet, no rap sheet. He just likes to spray-paint buildings."

"I know a couple of architects who'd like to spray-paint *him*," Captain Murtaugh growled. "Let's hope the media don't turn him into some sort of folk hero."

"They've already made a good start," she said dryly. "If you don't have anything for me, I'm going home."

"Go ahead." He waved her out.

Marian had a few things to clear up in her office before she could leave. *Her office*—a perk that came with her promotion. The novelty of having her own office following years of sitting in a squadroom had worn off about fifteen minutes after she'd moved in. The office itself was a small windowless cubicle, cramped for space, and in need of a good cleaning. But it had a door that could be closed when the noise level got unbearable, and it gave her a modicum of privacy as she oversaw the work of the twenty-five detectives in her charge at Midtown South Precinct. The detectives were supposed to be divided into three squads of seven or eight, each squad headed by a sergeant. But the unprecedented shortage of sergeants plaguing the police department had left Midtown South one sergeant short at the moment. The two sergeants oversaw squads of eleven and twelve each with Marian herself stepping in to help out when needed. The NYPD's newest lieutenant was earning her paycheck.

She'd been on the job only three weeks. But that was long enough to figure out which of her detectives resented taking orders from a woman and which were playing a waiting game. *Most* of them she had figured, that is; a couple she couldn't quite pin down. The two female detectives in the bunch appeared honestly glad to see a woman in the lieutenant's office; no problem there. And one of the men was a toady. Big smiles all the time, if you need any help let me know, my don't you look nice today. Jerk.

But they were all watching her, out of the corners of their eyes, waiting for her to make a mistake. Captain Murtaugh was watching too; he'd taken a chance, recommending her for promotion. If she screwed up, he'd look bad. Marian and the captain hadn't known each other long, had worked on only one case together while she was still technically attached to a different precinct. All of Midtown South was new to her—the personnel, the beat, the snitches, the danger spots, the ongoing rackets, the "flavors" of the area, the smells. She had a lot to learn.

Marian cleared her desk and put on her coat, pleased at getting away at a decent hour. She almost made it.

"Lieutenant Larch!" A young detective in shirtsleeves was talking on the phone and waving an arm at her.

She crossed the squadroom to his desk as he finished talking and hung up. O'Toole, his name was.

"This just in, Lieutenant," the detective said. "Passenger found dead on a crosstown bus. Caucasian male, in his seventies."

"Heart?"

"Bullet. Shot at close range. First officer says there's no telling how long he'd been riding like that. Dead, I mean." O'Toole cleared his throat. "Sergeant Campos isn't here."

Neither was anyone else. Campos was O'Toole's squad

leader, the one who made the case assignments. At the moment the young detective was the only one in the squad-room.

"Looks like you and me, O'Toole," Marian said. "Saddle up." So much for getting home early.

O'Toole grabbed his suit jacket and coat and followed her out.

* 3 *

The bus was sitting in the right-hand lane on West Thirty-fourth, directly in front of the West Side Jewish Center. Two uniformed officers were directing traffic around the obstacle, while another had the more demanding job of keeping a group of anxious, noisy people from pushing their way off the bus. The passengers were all crowded into the front half of the bus; the driver stood on the sidewalk beside the closed side door, talking to a fourth uniformed officer.

"Jesus!" said O'Toole. "How do you contain a crime scene like that?"

Marian was wondering the same thing herself. She started toward the bluesuit questioning the bus driver, but he saw her coming and said, "Stay back, ma'am."

She held up her shield. "Lieutenant Larch. Are you the first officer on the scene?"

His eyes widened a fraction: *So this is our new lady lieutenant.* "No, Lieutenant, Jackson's first officer." He indicated the bluesuit guarding the front exit of the bus. "What we gonna do about all these people?"

"We're going to let them off two at a time. What's your name, Officer?"

"Torelli." A pause. "Ma'am."

"Well, Torelli, I want you and Detective O'Toole here to take down the names and addresses of all the passengers and ask them if they saw anything."

"They all say they didn't see nothin'."

"Ask them again. If they have more than one form of ID, you can let them go. No ID or anything that smells fishy, hold them. For out-of-towners, get local addresses."

"I gotta call in," the bus driver said in an aggrieved tone.

"We'll call for you. Give the phone number to Detective O'Toole. And wait here—I'll want to talk to you."

The right bluesuit was guarding the bus passengers: a barrel-chested black man with shoulders wide enough to block the exit. "Officer Jackson?" Marian identified herself and told him to start letting the agitated passengers off two at a time. "You're the first officer?"

"Yes'm. Most of the passengers had scrammed before I got here. This bunch here musta been daydreaming—they didn't think nothing of it when the driver stopped the bus to make a phone call."

"I was afraid of that." She waited while Jackson ordered the first two passengers to step off; O'Toole and Torelli were waiting for them. "How long between the dispatcher's call and your arrival?"

"Couldna been more'n two or three minutes. But that's long enough for most of 'em to get off. There's only ten, twelve people here—but the driver said the bus was packed."

So most of their potential witnesses had disappeared into the streets. Marian nodded her thanks to Jackson and went back to the bus driver, who was watching the cops directing traffic around his bus amid a lot of horn-honking and shouting.

The driver was an angry man in his late thirties who took it as a personal affront that someone would go and get himself killed on *his* bus. "Like I don't have enough to worry about," he complained. "Busful of tired and short-tempered people on their way home from work. And me already behind schedule."

"How did you find out you had a dead man on board?" Marian asked. She had to shout to make herself heard.

"Passenger told me," the driver shouted back. "And she told me loud enough that everybody in the front part of the bus heard her. They couldn't wait to get out of there! I couldn't even go back and check the guy right away because of that mob pushin' to get off."

"Did you touch the body?"

"Hell, no. With all that blood everywhere? He was dead, all right."

"The woman who told you—was she one of those who left?"

The driver looked at her scornfully. "You expect her to hang around?"

No, Marian didn't. "I don't suppose you remember where the dead man got on?"

The driver looked smug. "Matter of fact, I do. Second Avenue."

"How can you be sure?"

"He was an old guy, slow . . . ya know. While he was climbin' on, I was lookin' at what the Thirty-Fourth East was showin'."

A movie theater. "So he was killed somewhere between Second and Ninth Avenues. Let's see, counting in Lexington and—"

"Nine blocks," he interrupted. "Exactly."

"And nobody heard the shot? Or saw anything?"

"Musta used a silencer," the driver said, nodding sagely.

While they'd been talking, both the Crime Scene Unit van and the car from the Medical Examiner's office had arrived. Marian could hear the CSU men griping about having to deal with a movable crime scene that was blocking traffic. They waited until the last passenger was off and then boarded the bus.

The traffic noise had died down to its usual level—which was to say, merely deafening. O'Toole and Torelli had let everyone go except three people, one of whom was a girl of thirteen or fourteen who looked scared to death. Marian shot a look at O'Toole.

"You said keep everybody who didn't have ID," he said defensively.

Marian drew the girl aside. "What's your name, kiddo?"

The girl whispered something.

"What's that? I can't hear you."

"Sharon Brandt." A louder whisper.

"Sharon, don't you know you should never leave home without carrying some kind of identification? What if you're in an accident? How could we let your parents know?"

The girl nodded dumbly, wide-eyed.

"Even if it's just a card you've written your address on. Something."

Sharon nodded again.

"You promise me you'll carry ID from now on?"

"Oh yes!" Faintly.

"Good. You go on home now."

The girl took off running. The other two who'd been held back were a middle-aged woman and a scruffy, stick-thin youngish man. The latter's pupils were pinpoints; his head was swaying in time to music only he could hear, and a loose grin made him appear as carefree as he probably felt. His only protection against the February cold was a ragged sweater; the guy looked like a slaphappy scarecrow.

"This one can't even tell us his name," O'Toole said in disgust.

Marian sighed. "Take him in and hold him until he comes down from wherever he is." Torelli led the unresisting scarecrow away.

That left the middle-aged woman, who blinked when a flash from the police photographer's camera went off inside the bus. She had short brown hair, minimal make-up, featureless clothing. Nondescript. "No ID?" Marian asked.

"Oh, she has ID all right," O'Toole said with a grim smile. "She's a private."

"I'm not licensed," the woman said hurriedly. "I *work* for a licensed detective. I'm an operative."

"Her name's Zoe Esterhaus," O'Toole added. "Zoh-ee without a *y*. She and the victim got on the bus at—"

"Second Avenue," Marian interrupted.

O'Toole looked surprised. "That's right."

Marian couldn't believe this early break. "You were following the victim?"

"Yes, I was," the operative admitted readily. "But don't ask me why. My instructions were to file a report on everywhere he went. That's all I know." The Esterhaus woman heaved a big sigh. "Lieutenant, I'd like to cooperate, but I really think you'd better talk to my boss."

"We're going to talk to both of you. What's the victim's name?"

"Oliver Knowles. Retired businessman of some sort. He lived on Central Park South. Lived pretty well, from what I could see."

"All right, Ms Esterhaus, I want you to go along to the station with Detective O'Toole. I'll be there shortly. O'Toole, get hold of her boss and have him come in. We'll need statements from both."

"You can't reach him now," the other woman said. "He's flying back from London tonight."

"Tomorrow, then. Call him first thing, O'Toole. But we'll get her statement first."

"Do you want me to take the car?" he asked. "How will you get back?"

"Take the car," Marian said. "Officer Jackson will give me a ride back, won't you, Officer?"

"Glad to, ma'am."

A man from the Crime Scene Unit was getting off the bus, carrying a battery-powered hand vacuum cleaner. "Do you have any idea," he said to the world at large, "how much *junk* is on the floor of a public bus?"

"Are you about finished?" Marian asked him.

"Yeah, we're done. Dr. Whittaker's still in there, though."

Marian climbed on the bus. She could see only the gray head of the victim leaning against the bus window, about three-fourths of the way back on the left as she faced the rear. The man from the Medical Examiner's office was bending over the body.

"Dr. Whittaker," Marian said, to let him know she was there.

He glanced over his shoulder. "Oh, hello, Sergeant Larch. Kind of off your turf, aren't you?"

"New precinct. And a new rank. It's Lieutenant Larch now."

"Congratulations," he said absently as he stood up straight. "You know, this guy's been dead less than an hour. Rigor's just starting."

Marian moved in and took a close look at Oliver Knowles's body. The dead man was wearing glasses and had a full iron-gray mustache. His overcoat looked expensive, and Marian could see the glint of a gold watch showing under the cuff of his left sleeve. His right hand was propping up a blood-soaked copy of *Newsweek* against his chest.

"Let's take a look at this," Dr. Whittaker said, easing the magazine out from under the dead man's hand. He held it up where light was showing behind it.

"No bullet hole," Marian said quickly. "Probably a contact shot?"

"Little hard to see powder burns under all that blood. The lab techs will have to look."

Marian nodded. "Bet you a dollar they're there. The killer held the gun to his chest, fired, and then propped up the magazine to hide the wound. He was probably off the bus and gone by the time the blood began seeping into the paper. Is that how you read it?"

"Sounds good to me, Sergeant," Dr. Whittaker said, having already forgotten her new title. "And I'll bet *you* a dollar that the bullet is so spread out in there we won't be able to identify the caliber."

"No bet," Marian said dryly. "But you'll let me know about the bullet right away? Before you go on with the autopsy?"

"First thing," he promised. "Anything else?"

"Pockets," she prompted.

With latex-gloved hands, Dr. Whittaker opened Knowles's blood-covered overcoat and went through his pockets, removing billfold, keys, coins, a wadded-up receipt slip from a drugstore, cigarettes, lighter, and an old-fashioned pearl-handled penknife. Marian bagged and tagged it all, including the dead man's eyeglasses and wristwatch.

"Gloves?"

He checked the overcoat pockets. "No gloves."

Odd. "Call me at Midtown South," she reminded Dr. Whittaker and made her way back up the aisle.

Outside, the temperature seemed to have dropped ten degrees during the short time she'd been on the bus. Marian pulled her coat tighter and headed toward where the Crime

Scene Unit van was waiting; the CSU was not permitted to remove anything from the body. Marian handed over her bags of evidence and said, "When Dr. Whittaker sends you the clothing, be sure to look for powder burns on the overcoat."

The CSU man looked annoyed. "We always do, Lieutenant."

Marian grinned and said, "And I want the victim's keys back first thing tomorrow morning. We'll need to get into his apartment."

"You got it."

She watched the body being removed from the bus. "What's your procedure when you have a movable crime scene? Do you take it with you?"

He shrugged and said, "We got no place to put a bus."

"I could tell the driver to take it back to the garage, if you need to go over it some more. Your call."

The CSU man shook his head. "It's a public bus. Six million fingerprints. We got everything in the immediate vicinity of the killing. You might as well let it go."

"Right." She stepped over to the bus driver and told him he could leave.

"About time," he grumbled and climbed aboard. The engine started up with a roar that made Marian flinch. The bus pulled away, followed by the CSU van and Dr. Whittaker's car.

A gust of wind made Marian shiver. She looked around for Officer Jackson.

"Ready to go, Lieutenant?" he said from behind her.

"Ready," she replied.

* 4 *

Zoe Esterhaus sat on a folding chair on the other side of a table from Marian in a Midtown South interview room, staring disconsolately at the slowly winding-and-unwinding double spool in the tape recorder. "I wish I could tell you more, Lieutenant Larch. I really do."

"So do I." The operative had had very little to add to what Marian already knew. "How many days had you been following him?"

"This is the fourth."

"What did he do with his time?"

"Stayed home, mostly. Too cold out for old bones, I guess. He went out to restaurants twice—alone. Like I said."

According to the woman who'd been hired to follow him, Oliver Knowles had taken a cab from his Central Park South apartment down to Lionel Madison Trains on East Twenty-third, where he'd stayed for thirty-five minutes. Then he'd taken another cab uptown eleven blocks to a store called Hobby World that had a GRAND OPENING sign in its window, along with an elaborate miniature train set. Knowles had stayed there for almost an hour. If he'd bought anything, he was having it delivered; he'd left both stores carrying nothing.

On the street immediately outside Hobby World, Knowles had searched through his overcoat pockets and then gone right back into the store again. When he came out the second time, he was still bare-handed.

But on Thirty-fourth Street, Knowles had not been able to get his third cab of the day. After ten minutes of trying, he'd given up and instead boarded the crosstown bus at Second Avenue. Zoe Esterhaus had boarded right behind him.

"Anyone else get on with you?" Marian asked.

"Four others. The bus was packed. The only reason Knowles got a seat was that two people got off at the next stop and he just happened to be standing nearest where they were sitting."

"*Two* people got off. Who sat down next to Knowles?"

"I couldn't see. I was standing in the aisle, a little farther back. Other people were between me and where Knowles sat down."

"And you didn't hear the shot?"

She shook her head. "The bus was noisy. I mean, the *bus* was noisy. It was one of those old ones that make so much noise your ears ring. The passengers weren't exactly quiet either. They were all pushing and snapping at one another. Bad scene."

"When did you learn he was dead?"

Esterhaus looked embarrassed. "Not until the police got there. The driver stopped the bus and most of the passengers got off. I didn't know what was going on, but I couldn't leave while Knowles was still there. He looked as if he was just resting his head against the window. I saw him only from the back, remember. I didn't know about the blood."

But enough others had known about it to get out of there as fast as they could. "And you never noticed anyone else following Knowles?"

This time she looked more than embarrassed; she looked

distraught. "No. I wasn't looking for anyone, but whoever was following Knowles was also following me. I should have caught that."

Marian stared at her in disbelief. Every private detective and operative she'd ever dealt with had always had a hundred excuses for everything he or she did or failed to do. It was like some honor code peculiar to the profession: Never admit to a mistake. Marian felt some urge to comfort Zoe Esterhaus. "You weren't hired to protect him. Only to watch."

"And a fine job I did of that. I didn't even see who shot him." She gave Marian a faint smile in acknowledgement of the latter's friendly gesture. "Not your problem."

Marian smiled back and turned off the tape recorder. "I'll get this typed up for you to sign. Can you think of anything else that might help us?"

Zoe Esterhaus slumped a little. "I wish to god I could."

Marian stepped out of the interview room and into the adjoining room where Captain Murtaugh stood looking through the one-way glass. "Anything?" she asked.

He shook his head. "I think you got everything. Let her go as soon as she signs her statement. I'll be in my office."

Marian went in search of a typist. The captain had come back to the station after leaving for the day, but at least he'd had some dinner. Marian's stomach growled.

A half hour later, Zoe Esterhaus had signed her statement and gone home. Marian got a cup of ersatz coffee out of the hall machine and took it with her to Captain Murtaugh's office.

"Dr. Whittaker just called," she told the captain after sitting down and taking a swallow of the let's-pretend coffee. "The slug mushroomed on impact and is not identifiable. Ballistics' guess is that it was a hand-load. And the lab found powder burns on the victim's overcoat."

Murtaugh nodded, a sour expression on his face; they both knew what they were dealing with here. "Spell it out," he ordered.

"A professional hit," she said, "obviously. Done in a crowded public place right under the nose of a trained observer. The killer follows Knowles without being spotted until the conditions are right. They get right, fast, on the bus. He slides into the seat next to Knowles with his gun concealed inside the copy of *Newsweek*. He's loaded his gun with dumdums or backward loads, and he's put a suppressor on the barrel. He presses the nozzle right up against Knowles's chest, muting the sound even more. One shot, and it's done. He slips the gun into his coat pocket, props up the magazine over the wound, and gets off the bus. Fast, neat, and anonymous. A paid-for murder."

Murtaugh stared at his hands glumly for a moment, and then said quietly, "A public bus. How coldly self-assured these killers are." He shifted his weight and asked, "Are you running this one yourself?"

"Yes." Marian gave up on the coffee and put the paper cup on the corner of Murtaugh's desk. "O'Toole caught the squeal, but he's too green to put in charge. I'll keep him on the case, though, and . . . oh, Perlmutter too, I suppose. To start."

"This may turn into a two-pronged investigation," Murtaugh cautioned. "Depending on whether the killer is a solo or not."

Marian nodded agreement. "Could be imported talent."

"Possibly."

Neither one of them wanted to think that Oliver Knowles's murderer was anything other than an independent killer for hire. Find out who hired him and they'd most likely get the guy who pulled the trigger as well. Case closed. But if there was a middleman, someone who kept a stable of talent available . . . this would be no simple murder investigation.

As if murder was ever simple.

Marian stood up tiredly. "We don't even know if Knowles had any family. I sent O'Toole to the apartment on Central Park South, but no one was there. That's the first order of business tomorrow. But right now, I'm going home."

"Larch."

"Yes, sir?"

"Don't forget your coffee."

In the car on the way home, Marian couldn't stop yawning. She thought about stopping for something to eat but decided to make do with whatever was in her refrigerator. She parked in her favorite place, the loading zone of a printing company that didn't open for business until after she'd left in the mornings. Upstairs in her apartment, the message light on her answering machine was blinking.

It was Kelly Ingram, who had no need to identify herself. "Hey, Marian, how about having a late supper with me? Puh-leeze? I'm so tired of hanging with these theayter types I could scream! Come on by after the performance."

Marian's closest friend, Kelly was a former television actor now starring in her first Broadway play. In the beginning it had been exciting, challenging, glamorous—all the things starring on Broadway was supposed to be. But gradually the sameness of what Kelly was doing began to pall . . . the same words every night, the same gestures, the same costumes. The same people. Kelly Ingram had a bad case of the fidgets.

Marian tapped out a number from memory. In a dressing room at the Broadhurst Theatre on Forty-fourth Street, a light on a telephone would start flashing in lieu of a ringing bell. Kelly's answering machine said: "Right now I'm out on the stage acting up a storm. Leave me a loving message, whoever you are."

After the beep, Marian said, "Hi, it's me. Forgive me, Kel, but I can't make it. I'm really bushed. It's ten-thirty and I just now got home from work." Six and a half hours late. "I'm going to take a long hot shower and make myself a sandwich and go to bed. You'll just have to put up with those the*ay*ter types a while longer, I suppose. Sorry, toots."

The shower felt good. Marian let the needle spray work on her neck and shoulders until the tension began to drain away. Looking at old men with bullet holes tended to wipe out whatever sense of well-being one might have built up during the day. No matter how many homicides Manhattan racked up, the newest one was always just as draining as the last.

She'd just stepped out of the shower when the door buzzer sounded. Marian slipped on a robe and padded over to the intercom. "Who is it?"

"Alberto's Gourmet Deli," said a static-laden voice.

"You have the wrong apartment. I didn't order anything."

"Marian Larch?"

"Yes, but—"

"I'm supposed to deliver a message. Kelly says don't start without her."

Marian sighed and buzzed him in.

* 5 *

"I don't know why they do that." Kelly Ingram poked a fork at her plate in annoyance. "There's chicken, and sesame seed, and that little weed looks like thyme. But all you can taste is cayenne! Why do they do that?"

"I really don't know," Marian answered soberly. "Here, try some of this. It's good."

Kelly peered suspiciously into the deli carton. "What is it?"

"No idea." Marian laughed. "Hey, you ordered the stuff!"

"I asked for an assortment." Kelly adventurously spooned out some of the mystery mixture and tried it. "Hm, that *is* good. Shrimp something, I think. Maybe."

"I'm sorry we couldn't go out."

"Ho, this is better," Kelly said. "No fans to gawk at you while you're trying to eat. Especially one fan. Ugh."

"One in particular? Kelly . . . are you being stalked?"

"God, no—nothing like that! There's just this one girl who seems to be *everywhere* I go. I know she comes to the theater every night, and every night when I leave she tells me she's my number-one fan. But she's no stalker. She's too wimpy for that."

"You sure?"

"Positive."

"Okay, then," Marian said. "So, how'd it go tonight?"

"Terrific. They loved us. Same as always."

"How teddibly boring for you."

"Well, it is," Kelly said earnestly. "Oh, I know it's great the play's still going strong . . . eighteenth week! But if something *different* would only happen once in a while! If we could change the blocking, or if Ian would forget his lines, or . . . something!"

"You don't really want Ian to forget his lines." Ian Cavanaugh was Kelly's leading man, a long-established star who'd probably never forgotten his lines once in his entire professional life.

"It'd serve him right. He's been grumpy as a bear lately."

"Why?"

"I think he misses Abby."

Abigail James had written *The Apostrophe Thief*, the play that Kelly Ingram and Ian Cavanaugh were starring in. It wasn't the first role she'd written expressly for Ian, nor would it be the last; the two of them shared a brownstone and a life as well as a profession. At the moment Abby was attending script conferences in California, preparing for the movie version of the play. After playing hard-to-get for an acceptable period of time, both Kelly and Ian had signed contracts to repeat their roles on film.

"Are you excited about the movie?" Marian asked.

"Not yet. But I will be when the time comes." Kelly opened a square bakery box and lifted out a cheesecake. "Ta-taa!"

Marian groaned. "Oh god, no."

"What do you mean oh-god-no? You love cheesecake."

"Kelly, I can't eat everything I see and never put on an ounce, the way you do. Why, I gained five pounds the minute you opened that box!"

"Make up for it tomorrow. Steamed vegetables." Kelly cut a wedge of the cheesecake, put it on a plate, and pushed it over toward Marian. "Treat yourself for putting in such a long day. Why did you put in such a long day?"

"New homicide," Marian said shortly.

Kelly slowly lowered her fork. "Oh. You looked at a dead person today." She was silent a moment. Then: "You looked at a dead person, and I come in here kvetching about too much cayenne in the chicken. God, Marian, I'm sorry."

Marian waved a hand dismissively. "Don't be. You can't ask me if I've just looked at a body every time you see me before you know how to talk to me. It's just that this one . . . well, a man in his seventies was shot on a bus this afternoon. On a crowded public *bus*, Kelly. And nobody saw or heard a thing."

She understood immediately. "A contract killing."

"Has to be. And get this. The victim was being followed by a private operative, who also saw and heard nothing."

"Wow. You mean a private detective was right there on the bus at the time of the murder?"

"Yep, except operatives aren't licensed detectives. They do the leg work for detectives—tracking stuff down in the Municipal Archives, tailing people, like that."

"And he didn't see anything?"

"Not a thing. And it's a she, by the way."

"A woman operative, huh. Is that usual?"

"Not very. But this one has the right look for a good operative. Nondescript, the sort of person you never notice. Just what you want for tail jobs."

"How old is she?"

"Oh, late forties, early fifties."

Kelly nodded. "The age women become invisible."

Marian shot her friend an appreciative look. "I hadn't thought of that. I wonder if that's why her boss hired her in the first place—oh hell!"

"What?"

"O'Toole forgot to tell me the name of the agency that employs her . . . and I forgot to ask."

"Big deal, so you find out tomorrow. Who's O'Toole? A police detective?"

Marian said yes. "A young one, and a new one. He's been a detective only about a week longer than I've been a lieutenant. We're the two greenhorns in the precinct."

Kelly hooted. "Oh yeah, you're *real* green, Lieutenant Larch!"

"I'm green at lieutenant-ing. And this is my first big-case homicide since I moved up in rank. So I've got to nail this one."

"Any reason to think you won't?"

"Too early to say."

They both concentrated on their cheesecake for a minute or two. "Why," Kelly finally asked, "is an old man on a bus such a threat that someone would be driven to hiring a killer?"

"That's what I start working on tomorrow," Marian said.

* 6 *

Detectives O'Toole and Perlmutter sat facing Marian in her office. Two more unalike police detectives she couldn't imagine. O'Toole was young and fresh-faced, looking as if he were about to burst into song at any minute. The very cliché of the eager new detective. Perlmutter, on the other hand, could easily be mistaken for the editor of an avant-garde intellectual journal that only ten people in the entire country ever read. Thin, bushy-haired, wearing wire-rim glasses, Perlmutter had something professorial about his manner. He should be a good partner for O'Toole.

"The first thing we do," Marian said, "is find out if Oliver Knowles had any family. Captain Murtaugh didn't release Knowles's name to the news media pending notification of next of kin, so let's do some notifying." She dropped the victim's set of keys on the desk. "The lab just sent these over. There's bound to be something in his apartment. Finish this up fast."

Perlmutter nodded and scooped the keys up off the desk. "You want to talk to him or her or them, whatever?"

Marian nodded. "Say I'll be around this afternoon. See what you can find out about what the victim had been up to lately . . . but don't push too hard, give them time to recover if they need it. Use your own judgement. They'll want to know about the body—Dr. Whittaker says they can have it tomorrow."

"Credit cards?" Perlmutter asked.

"He didn't have any." Both men looked surprised. "What can I tell you?" Marian said. "Knowles was a cash man. But see if you can find a checkbook."

O'Toole spoke up. "What about fingerprints?"

"Not in our system. I've put in a request to the FBI, but don't count on anything there. Knowles seems to have lived his seventy years or so without any contact with the police at all. We've got nothing on him."

"Bullet?" Perlmutter asked. "Flattened, I suppose."

"Unfortunately. It did enter at an angle that suggests the shooter held the gun in his left hand."

"Well, that's something!" O'Toole said. "At least we know the killer's left-handed."

"No, we don't," Perlmutter told him. "Most professional hitters are ambidextrous when it comes to handling their weapons."

O'Toole looked a question at Marian; she nodded. "Also, no fingerprints on the magazine that was propped up in the victim's lap, not even the victim's. The shooter brought the mag with him."

Perlmutter said, "After we talk to next of kin, what?"

"Depends on what I find out this morning. Call in. That's all for now." The two detectives stood up. "O'Toole, stay a moment. Ask Sergeant Campos to step in here, will you, Perlmutter?"

"He's in court this morning. The Hysinger case."

"I thought that was supposed to finish yesterday afternoon?"

Perlmutter shrugged I-don't-know and left. Marian turned her attention to O'Toole. "This is your first homicide, isn't it?"

"Yes, ma'am!" Rarin' to go.

"I want you to listen carefully to Perlmutter. He has good instincts, O'Toole. Even when he's just thinking out loud, listen to him. *Especially* when he's thinking out loud."

"Yes, ma'am!" Getting more antsy by the second.

"Don't go off on your own. Any line of investigation that occurs to you, you check with Perlmutter first. Understood?"

"Yes, ma'am!" O'Toole was practically dancing, he was so eager to get going.

Marian sighed. "Oh, go." He went. She'd save the full lecture for later.

A head peered around the doorjamb. "You got time for me?"

"Sure, Buchanan. Come in."

The next half hour was spent listening to Sergeant Buchanan bring her up to date on the cases his squad was investigating. She asked a few questions, made a suggestion or two; but on the whole she was content to leave it all in Buchanan's hands. Next to Captain Murtaugh, he was the most experienced cop at Midtown South.

"That's all," Sergeant Buchanan said. "Except for one that ain't ours—I sent it to Missing Persons. Female graduate student at NYU, Robin Muller, age twenty-two . . . just dropped out of sight. I got a bad feeling about this one."

"Why?"

"Boyfriend reported her missing. He says the last few months, she's had more money than she used to have, and she wouldn't tell him where it came from. Not a whole lot of more money, but enough to make things easier. Like, when it's her turn to spring for a meal, it's dinner in a restaurant instead of hot dogs on the corner. And she'd run up a big phone bill and then pay it." He held up a meaty hand, as if to stop Marian from interrupting. "Boyfriend's sure she ain't hookin' because she's with him every night. And she's kind of a health nut—no drugs. But she just didn't come back to their place one afternoon. It don't look good."

"No," Marian agreed. "You called the morgue? Has anyone fitting her description—"

"Naw, I checked. But she was into somethin' she shouldna been. I'm gonna keep an eye out. If it's okay with you, Lieutenant."

Marian said it was, well aware that he would have done so whether she okayed it or not. "Where do they live? Near NYU?"

"Lafayette Street. Ninth Precinct, if that's what you're thinkin'."

"That's what I'm thinking. Why'd he come to us?"

"Spur of the moment. Walkin' down Thirty-fifth, saw the station, decided to come in."

Marian nodded. "Let me know if she turns up."

Buchanan left and Marian quickly shifted gears back to the Oliver Knowles killing. Knowles's billfold had contained four-hundred-fifty dollars, a driver's license, and a photograph of a white Persian cat. *At least there was a cat in his life*, Marian thought. It was unusual to find a billfold that told so little of the owner's personal life. It was almost as if Knowles didn't want to give away anything about himself.

A crumpled drugstore receipt had been in his pocket. It showed that he'd bought a carton of cigarettes six days earlier . . . before Zoe Esterhaus had started following him. Marian was sure there was nothing more to learn from Esterhaus; the woman had told them everything she knew, which was precious little. Marian hoped her boss would—

Esterhaus's boss. He was coming in this morning.

She left her office and stepped over to the nearest desk in

the squadroom, where a detective was typing up a report. "Dowd, I'm expecting a private investigator. I don't know his name, but he's Zoe Esterhaus's employer."

"Esterhaus, gotcha. Uh, that's the private op who was on the bus?"

"That's the one. Let me know the minute her boss gets here."

"Right."

"I'll be at the holding cell." She made her way to where one corner of a room crowded with file cabinets was boxed off with hurricane fencing. Inside the cage the druggie scarecrow they'd taken off the bus the day before had come down from his high; he was sitting on a cot with his head in his hands, moaning out loud.

Two bluesuits lounged casually outside the cell, watching him and laughing. One of them, named McAndrew, said to the other, "You know how to say 'Hi' to an addict? You flick his nose gently with your finger and watch him scream." Both men guffawed.

"Cute, McAndrew, real cute," Marian said. The laughter stopped. "Do you have the key to this thing? Open up."

McAndrew unlocked the holding cell and Marian stepped inside. The scarecrow looked up at her and said, "I need something, man."

"Uh-huh. Answer a question or two and you'll be out of here."

"'Bout what?"

"About the man who was shot on the bus yesterday."

He squinted his eyes. "What man?"

"You don't know a man was shot?"

But he was still thinking about her original question. "What bus?"

"You don't remember being on the crosstown bus, about four-thirty, quarter to five, yesterday afternoon?"

He just shook his head. "I tell you, I need something."

Marian sighed; start at the beginning. "What's your name?"

"Nolan Baker."

"Where do you live, Nolan?"

"I'm staying with a friend." He gave her a name and address. "I was on a bus yesterday?"

"That's right. You don't remember?"

"I never ride the bus. I always take the subway or walk. What was I doing on a bus?"

"Going from one place to another, I presume. Come on, Nolan, think. Where had you been? Where's the last place you remember?"

Suddenly he got cagey. "What do you want to know that for?"

Marian looked at the wreck of a human being sitting before her and knew what he was afraid of. "Nolan, listen carefully. I'm not trying to find your supplier. That's not what this is about. But a man was murdered on the same bus you were riding, and I want to know if you saw anything. Try to remember."

He shook his head. "I don't remember no bus."

Reluctantly, Marian decided she believed him. She motioned to McAndrew to let her out. "Kick him loose," she instructed.

Back in the squadroom she said "Not here yet?" to Detective Dowd as she passed his desk.

"Not yet."

At her own desk, she wrote down Nolan Baker's name and address before she forgot them, for the record. Then she started making a list of things to check. The two stores Knowles had visited yesterday, for starters. See if he had bought anything to be delivered later. Did he pay cash? Did he have private accounts, since he carried no credit cards? If Knowles was a long-time customer at Lionel Madison Trains, possibly the clerks would know something about him. He'd left his gloves either there or in one of the cabs he'd taken, but so what? There really was nothing to go on yet, not until Perlmutter and O'Toole had finished searching his apartment.

At least she knew that Knowles had liked model trains. And cats. His address, his expensive clothes, and his semi-expensive hobby all told her he wasn't hurting for money. The lack of personal items in his billfold suggested . . . caution? Wariness? Or perhaps Knowles was just an old man who had withdrawn from the world. But if that was the case, why did someone want him dead? Did he control a lot of money?

Detective Dowd interrupted her musings. "Hey, Lieutenant, that private eye is here—Esterhaus's boss."

"Good. Send him in."

She made a note to herself of several avenues of investigation that might tell them something of Knowles's finances; money had been behind almost every murder she had investigated since she first earned her gold shield. Marian was aware of someone stepping into her office; she finished writing and looked up.

"You rang?" said Curt Holland.

* 7 *

He stood there in the doorway of Marian's office as if he owned it: the King of Manhattan bestowing a regal favor. His clothes were fresh and costly-looking, as they always were. Expensive gray business suit and tie; Marian had never seen him in a tie before. But deep shadows lay under his eyes. Zoe Esterhaus had said he was flying back from London last night . . . jet lag, then. Or a more general weariness.

"What were you doing in London?" she asked abruptly.

"Tending to business."

Meaning it's none of mine, she thought. Marian had almost forgotten how thick and soft his hair was. She hadn't seen Holland in over a month; he could be up to anything, as far as she knew. It might even be legal. "Playing it close to the vest? What a surprise."

"I strive for consistency."

"You succeed."

They both fell silent, challenging each other. Marian stared back as his black eyes never left hers—reminding her, questioning her, daring her. Exhausting her. Curt Holland was not a man one could ignore. Marian had tried.

At least it was encouraging to discover that she had not the slightest urge to jump up and rip his clothes off. Not the slightest. No. "We're going to have to work together," she told him simply. "There's no way around it."

He gave her the sardonic smile that she hated. "But I'm sure you looked long and hard to find one."

Damn him. "Holland, I didn't know you were Zoe Esterhaus's boss until you stepped into that doorway!"

"Now tell me another."

"Believe it or not . . . I don't much care. Why do I always end up justifying myself to you?"

He gave in, a little. "I do believe it. You've never lied to me. Why do I always end up apologizing to you?"

Marian was silent a moment, letting him work that one out for himself. She looked away from those high cheekbones a model would kill for and concentrated on the matter at hand. "We have police business to take care of," she said with finality. "So let's take care of it. Esterhaus filled you in on what happened?"

In response, he raised one arm in an extravagant Elizabethan gesture, indicating the chair facing her desk. "May I?"

Marian merely nodded, not rising to the bait; Holland was never more courteous than when her own manners suffered a lapse. "You know how Oliver Knowles died?"

Holland seated himself and said, "Gunshot wound, administered on a crosstown bus in the midst of a crowd of unseeing passengers, one of whom was my operative. Contract, of course."

"Who hired you to have Knowles followed?"

"I don't know."

"Holland—"

"Hear me out," he said quickly. "I really don't know." He sighed. "I have in my employ a brilliant young hacker named André Flood, who knows more about computing than I do. Nineteen years old and two college degrees. He handles much of our computer-related investigations—"

"*He* does? But that's your turf."

Holland grunted. "I've decided I don't want to spend the rest of my life staring at a computer screen," he replied testily. "Don't interrupt. André knows all there is to know about computers, but he still has a great deal to learn about the way a private investigation agency operates."

"He took the case."

Holland nodded. "My own plans had changed rather quickly—I had to leave for London a day earlier than I'd planned. I called the office from JFK and André was the only one there. Shortly after I called, a woman came in and paid a cash retainer to have Oliver Knowles followed. André called Zoe—who thought the orders were coming from me, since André neglected to tell her I was already on my way to London." He sighed. "I'd be surprised if André gave the matter a second thought. He undoubtedly resented being taken away from his computer even long enough to get her to sign a contract."

"Name on the contract?"

"Laura Cisney." He spelled it. "But it's false. And her address is a phony too. André and I spent the morning searching through bank records, the DMV, Social Security, and so on—nothing. There's no such person as Laura Cisney."

Marian was not at all pleased by this reminder that Holland could access supposedly secure electronic records with such ease. "What did she look like?"

"Medium."

She stared. "That's it? Medium?"

Holland spread his hands. "According to André. Medium height, medium weight, medium hair, medium eyes . . . I asked him what color medium eyes are, and he flapped his hands and said, 'Oh, you know—*medium.*' "

Marian shook her head. "Not good enough. Get him in here, Holland. I'll put him with one of the portrait people and they can build a face."

"I'll send him in, but don't count on much." A corner of his mouth twisted. "André is not . . . the most observant young man in the world. He introduced himself to Zoe three times before she got tired of it and started wearing a name tag in the office."

"Huh. I hope your André isn't badgering you to go out on a case."

"Fortunately, no. The very thought terrifies him."

"Where'd you find this guy?"

A slow smile. "I looked for him."

His nice smile. "Then he must be dynamite with a computer," Marian said.

"That he is."

"Is there anything else?" she asked. "Do you know anything more at all that might help us get started?"

"I'm sorry to say I don't. But I'd like to make up for this absence of specifics. I feel a certain embarrassment at the lack of professionalism my agency displayed when I was not here to ride herd on everybody. Any way I can help, just say the word."

Marian considered. There were many things about Curt Holland that she didn't trust, but his efficiency was not one of them. Maybe she could save the city a few bucks. "This electronic search you made for Laura Cisney—how thorough was it?"

"Pretty thorough. There are a few places left to look, though."

"Look there, then? And let me know what you find?"

"Certainly. Always happy to save the city a dollar or two."

She glowered, hating to be so transparent. "That's all, then. Thanks for coming in."

There was a brief pause, after which Holland announced to the world at large: "I am dismissed. The lieutenant has spoken." He pronounced it *lefftenant*.

He stood up and moved to the door, where he assumed a military posture and bowed stiffly. "What the lieutenant wishes, the lieutenant gets."

Marian smiled. "And don't you forget it," she said mildly.

* 8 *

It was lunchtime before Perlmutter called in. "Oliver Knowles was a widower. One son—Austin Knowles, an architect. We tracked him down at a construction site on Wall Street. He didn't tell us anything—he was pretty broken up, Lieutenant."

"Where is he now?" Marian asked.

"Went home." He read off a Fifth Avenue address. "I told him you'd be along later. But Oliver Knowles had a cook-housekeeper, Ellen Rudolph—and she was pretty broken up too. Widow, lives in. But she did tell us Knowles was a retired toy manufacturer. There's one more person living in the apartment, Knowles's secretary . . . name of Lucas Novak. But he's in Florida this week. Family matter, Mrs. Rudolph said."

Marian wrote down *Austin Knowles, Mrs. Ellen Rudolph, Lucas Novak.* "Didn't Mrs. Rudolph wonder when Knowles didn't come home last night?"

"She didn't know. She's just getting over the flu, and Knowles had told her he'd fend for himself until she felt better. She hadn't left her suite for a couple of days."

"Suite?"

"Yeah, suite. That housekeeper lives better than I do. Lucas Novak has his own suite too. And two whole rooms of the apartment are given over to an elaborate model-train layout, Mrs. Rudolph says. You gotta see that place, Lieutenant."

"I intend to." Live-in help—money money money. "Did you ask the housekeeper to let you look around?"

Perlmutter hesitated. "No, I didn't. The lady's sick, Lieutenant, and she's upset by Knowles's death. Besides, I thought we ought to notify the son before we did anything else."

"You did right," Marian said. "In the meantime, I want you to go to Lionel Madison Trains on East Twenty-third and that new place . . ." She looked through her notes. "Hobby World on Thirty-fourth Street. Find out if Knowles ever came in with anybody, and how he paid for his purchases. Get some more names, Perlmutter."

"Do my best," he said. "What about the private that was following Knowles?"

"A probable dead end," Marian told him. "I'll fill you in when you get back." She said goodbye and hung up.

Marian added her notes to Knowles's file. So Knowles had made toys for a living—evidently a very lucrative living, since he obviously was well-heeled at the time of his death. And he'd spent his retirement years playing with trains. Was he on good terms with his son? Why did a retired toymaker need a secretary? Did he have any regular visitors? Where else did he go besides model-train stores when he went out?

She checked the time and headed for Captain Murtaugh's office, hoping to catch him before he left for lunch. She was in luck; the captain was poring over a report but waved her in.

"What have you got on the bus killing?" he asked.

Marian brought him up to date, sketching out what she planned to do next. "At this point I'd be tempted to consider the possibility that the shooter got the wrong man—if it weren't for the fact that someone hired a private to tail Knowles. *Something* was going on."

"The man had money," Murtaugh said. "There's your motive."

Marian was inclined to agree. "So far, nothing else about his life seems to explain an act of murder. But we're just getting started."

"This woman who wanted him followed—how does she fit in?"

"Don't know yet. She couldn't be the one who paid for the hit—why would she go to a private investigator for a simple tail job, then? Could be the two aren't connected at all."

"You think that's likely?"

"No. But it's possible. You know we probably won't find her, don't you?"

The captain didn't like that. "This hacker who's the only one who saw her . . . he can't give us anything at all?"

"I haven't talked to him yet, but Holland says he's pretty unobservant."

"Let's not take Holland's word for it, shall we?" Murtaugh said dryly. He and Holland had met a couple of times; the two didn't exactly hit it off. "When's this André coming in?"

"He may be here now. I called in a technician from the Graphic Arts Unit." Like many cops, Marian was herself trained in the use of Identakit, the book of manual plastic overlays of mouths, eyes, hairstyles, etc.; but the result was always a line drawing. Computer programs could build a portrait the same way and then morph the drawing into a recognizable human face. "I left word I wanted to see him after he finishes with the portrait."

Murtaugh nodded. "Keep me posted." He turned back to the report he'd been reading.

Marian started out but hesitated. "Captain?"

He didn't look up. "Something else?"

She hesitated again, but then blurted out: "Captain Murtaugh, have you ever been the best man in a wedding?"

That got his attention. Surprised, he said, "As a matter of fact, I have. My brother's wedding, in Pittsburgh—oh, a good twenty years ago. Why?"

Marian sighed. "My former partner is getting married." This next part was awkward. "And he's asked me to be his best man."

Captain Murtaugh stared . . . and then barked a laugh. "You? Best *man*?"

She sighed again. "Preposterous, isn't it? But Ivan says there's no other place for me in the ceremony. I've only just met the bride, so I can't be a member of *her* party. I might add that Ivan is getting a lot of fun out of this."

Murtaugh laughed again. "I met him, didn't I? Sergeant up in the Three-two? I forget his last name."

"Malecki. Ivan Malecki. What I want to know is . . . what am I supposed to do? I know I have to make sure Ivan and the ring both make it to the church—but what else? Ivan's no help. He's too busy cracking jokes about the best man at his wedding to give me any straight answers. But when the time comes, he's going to be panic-stricken and start thinking of all these little details that haven't been taken care of and . . . well, you see the problem. Do you mind telling me what you did at your brother's wedding?"

The captain was leaning back in his chair, grinning at her. "You do have interesting problems, Larch. Well, let's see. What did I do as best man? It's been a while. Hm . . . I had to make sure everyone in the wedding party had transportation from the church to where the reception was being held."

"Oh my," Marian said and took out her notebook and started writing.

·

"And the best man is traditionally in charge of the ushers. Make sure they know what they're supposed to do, like that."

Marian groaned.

"You know you're supposed to toast the bride and groom at the reception?"

"Yes, I know about that."

"Oh . . . and I remember I had to pay everybody who got paid," the captain went on. "My brother gave me a bunch of envelopes with checks in them, and it was up to me to pay the caterers, the organist—is there going to be an organist?"

"I have no idea," Marian said faintly.

"Musicians at the reception? They'll have to be paid. And the priest—don't forget the . . . minister? Rabbi?"

"Priest," she said. "I'm not Catholic. Will that cause problems?"

"Naw. You just won't take part in the prenuptial confession, that's all." Suddenly he sat up straight. "You know what you should do? Have you met the bride's mother?"

"Not yet."

"Then go introduce yourself. Enlist her help. It's always the mother who runs these things anyway. She'll tell you exactly what's expected of you."

Marian brightened. "That's a good idea! Thanks, Captain! That's just what I'll do. Oh lord, I'll be glad when this is over."

"Hey, you'll have a great time. You'll see."

"If I don't kill Ivan first."

"You can always refuse."

"I did. I told him I'd be perfectly happy just to be a guest at his wedding. But he wouldn't hear of it. He just kept on and on at me about it and . . . well, he wore me down. And now I'm stuck."

Murtaugh was laughing again. He was still laughing when Marian got up and went back to her own office.

The detectives' squadroom was busy. About three-fourths of the desks were occupied, phones were ringing, and most of the extra chairs had been taken by victims, suspects, witnesses—all talking loudly, straining to make themselves heard over the racket. It was bound to happen; the morning had been too quiet.

Marian was thinking about lunch when she saw someone was waiting in her office—a woman in her late twenties, dark hair pulled straight back and fastened at the nape. Sharp clothes. She stood up when Marian walked in.

"Lieutenant Larch? My name is Paula Dancer—I'm from the Graphic Arts Unit. I was just working with André Flood on a portrait of a woman he's supposed to identify?"

"Ah, good. Did you finish?"

"Uh, yes, we finished it."

"Then what's the problem? Why didn't you just send it up?"

"I thought I'd better bring it to you myself." She opened a folder and took out the computer-generated portrait.

Marian looked at the portrait . . . and then looked back at Paula Dancer. "That's you!"

Dancer nodded slowly, a wry smile on her face. "Just as a test, I asked André to describe the man he works for. We built up a perfect likeness of the man sitting at the next desk."

Marian made a noise of exasperation. "Do you have that one with you?"

"Uh—yes." She fished another portrait out of her folder. "Do you know him?"

"I know the man André works for." Marian looked at the portrait. "And he doesn't look *anything* like that! Christ."

Dancer smiled in sympathy. "I'm afraid our André is easily distracted. I thought you ought to know."

"Thanks, I appreciate it. Where is our wonderful witness now?"

"He's out in the squadroom. Shall I send him in?"

"Please."

Dancer grinned. "You know, I think that's the first time anyone has said 'please' to me since I joined the force. I'll go get André." She left.

André Flood, when he came in, was a surprise. Like most people, Marian had a mental picture of a computer hacker as someone overweight, unkempt, with bad skin. A can of Coke in one hand and a bag of munchies in the other. But that must have been the first generation of hackers; Holland's André was, in contrast, exceedingly kempt. Jacket and tie, good haircut, and a perfect baby-boy face that must drive the girls wild. He called Marian "ma'am" and avoided eye contact.

When he was seated across from her, Marian pushed the two sketches toward him that Paula Dancer had left. "The man first," she said. "You maintain that's an accurate representation of your boss?"

The young man picked up the computer-generated sketch and examined it carefully. "There are some differences, but—essentially, yes."

"Essentially, no," Marian said. "The only similarities between that face and Holland's are that they're both male and they're both clean-shaven. And they both have dark hair. The graphics tech told me that's the face of the detective who was sitting at the next desk."

"Really?" André found this mildly interesting.

"How can you not know what the man you work for looks like?"

He looked everywhere in the room except at Marian. "I do know what Mr. Holland looks like. I'm just not very good at describing people."

"I'll say. This sketch of the woman is useless."

"Excuse me, ma'am, but I'm pretty sure of that one."

Marian sighed. "André, do you remember the police-woman who composed these pictures? You last saw her, oh, three minutes ago."

"Uh, I remember her," he answered vaguely.

She flicked the sketch with her finger. "There she is."

His eyes widened, his attention caught at last. "I described the policewoman? Wow. Isn't it amazing, the tricks your mind plays on you?"

"Yeah, really amazing." Marian turned both sketches facedown and tried to get him to look at her. "Think back, André. What were you doing when this woman calling her-self Laura Cisney came into the office?"

"Well, I was tracing funds a building contractor was mov-ing around to keep them from being frozen by the IRS. He was using South American banks mostly—"

"The IRS hired Holland's agency?"

"No, one of the contractor's creditors is our client. I don't think I should talk about it, ma'am. Confidentiality, you know."

"Oh." Marian suppressed a smile. "So you were trying to trace the movement of this contractor's money. Where were you? Physically."

He looked faintly surprised at the question. "In my office." *Like, where else?*

"How did you know when this woman came in?"

"She didn't come in, at first—the door's kept locked. She pressed a buzzer and my security light started to flash. It was my week to cover when the receptionist went to lunch.

So I looked at the monitor and saw it was just a woman, alone."

Just a woman. "So you buzzed her in. Then what?"

Marian took him through the encounter step by step. André told her what he could, his eyes fixed throughout on some spot in the vicinity of her left ear. It became clear that André had paid no more attention to Laura Cisney's face than he was paying to Marian's now. She got the distinct impression that Holland's young computer genius was giving her maybe one percent of his attention. He was just going through the motions of being interviewed because Holland had ordered him to come in; but his mind was elsewhere. *Probably in South America,* Marian thought. When she'd asked all the questions she could think to ask, she still had nothing more than André's original description of the woman who wanted Oliver Knowles followed: she was medium.

Finally she said, "I'm disappointed, André. I was hoping you'd be able to help us."

"I'm sorry."

But he wasn't, Marian thought, watching him watching the wall behind her head. He wasn't sorry and he wasn't even interested. André wasn't being uncooperative; he just wasn't . . . here. Whatever problem Marian had, it was hers alone; he was totally detached from it. Marian speculated over whether he wasn't responding to her because: a) she was a police lieutenant; b) she was female; c) she was not of his generation; d) she didn't live her life through computers. She suspected the answer was d).

At last she let him go, wondering if he'd recognize her the next time he saw her.

* 9 *

Mrs. Austin Knowles opened the door to Marian's ring. Redhead, in her late thirties, her pretty face drawn into tight lines of distress. She was wearing a ruffled peach blouse with slim black trousers; something green sparkled at her earlobes. Marian introduced herself and was invited in after only a momentary hesitation.

"Austin is lying down," Mrs. Knowles explained, offering Marian a seat on a white sofa as long as Marian's kitchen. She herself sat on a facing black sofa, equally long and about ten feet away. Marian could visualize a party in this room—*Oh, do come in . . . I think there's a place left on the black sofa.* Two rows of people talking at each other over a ten-foot space. Marian put the image out of her head and murmured a conventional expression of sympathy.

"This is very hard for Austin," Mrs. Knowles said, "losing both parents so close together."

"His mother died recently?"

"Just last month. It was cancer . . . a long, drawn-out illness."

"I'm sorry." Marian let a moment pass and then said, "Mrs. Knowles, do you have any idea why someone would want your father-in-law dead?"

She shook her head. "I have to think the . . . the killer

shot the wrong man. Oliver was just an old man who liked to play with toys."

"But he was a wealthy old man. Who inherits all that?"

Mrs. Knowles flared. "Are you accusing my husband?"

Marian tried to look startled. "No. I'm asking a question. I'm assuming your husband is the main beneficiary, but was anyone else named in the will?"

The woman looked uncertain. "You'd better ask Austin."

"All right, I will. I'm sorry to disturb Mr. Knowles, but I do need to talk to him now."

Mrs. Knowles frowned. "I'll go see if he's awake." She left the room.

The Knowleses lived well. From what Marian could see of their Fifth Avenue apartment, the architecturing biz was paying off handsomely for Austin Knowles. This whole family was used to having money. And if the money stayed in the family, maybe the motive behind the killing was something else.

Austin Knowles came in looking haggard and grim, obviously hit hard by his father's death. The manner of the old man's dying was enough to rock anyone, but following so soon after his mother's death . . . Marian felt a stab of sympathy for the architect. Since Mrs. Knowles had not returned with her husband, Marian once again introduced herself. Knowles sat down at the opposite end of the long white sofa.

He was a slim, tense man in his forties who walked leaning forward . . . blue eyes, blond hair beginning to thin on top. In normal times he probably carried an air of authority. But in the midst of grieving for his father, Knowles seemed disoriented, uncertain. "Do you have a line on the killer yet?" he asked before Marian could start the interview.

"No," Marian answered regretfully. "We're not going to get any leads from those people on the bus, Mr. Knowles.

They didn't see anything. We're going to have to look for whoever hired him."

Knowles rubbed a hand over his mouth. "Why? He was a harmless old man. Why would anyone want to kill him?"

"That's what I was hoping you could tell me. Let's get the unpleasant part out of the way first. Who inherits?"

"I do. Trust funds set up for his secretary and his house-keeper, but I get the bulk of it."

"How big are the trust funds?"

"Big enough to give them both a comfortable income for the rest of their lives. But both Lucas—ah . . ."

"Lucas Novak and Mrs. Ellen Rudolph, yes."

Knowles nodded. "You know about them, right. But they're family, Lieutenant. Lucas and Mrs. R and Dad had been living comfortably together for nearly twenty years. Well, Mrs. R has been there twenty years . . . I guess it's more like fifteen for Lucas. But they were both protective of Dad. They took care of him. Neither one of them would want him dead."

"Isn't that unusual, leaving trust funds for people who are, well . . ."

"Getting along in years? Yes, it is. But Dad asked them whether they'd like a lump sum or a steady income, and they both opted for the latter."

"So he talked about his will with them. When was this?"

"Oh, four or five years ago. Dad always took care of his people, and he always let them know where they stood. But even though Mrs. R and Lucas won't have any financial wor-ries, they are going to lose their home. That won't be easy for them, after so many years."

"You inherit the apartment? And you're going to sell it?"

"Oh yes. It's a valuable piece of real estate, Lieutenant. I'm not going to do anything about it until I'm sure Mrs. R and Lucas are settled somewhere, though. I haven't had time to think about these things yet. But those two would never do anything that would cost them their home. It's absurd even to consider it."

Marian reserved judgement, but the flat way Knowles had closed the subject told her there was no point in pursuing it now. Look elsewhere. "Did your father sell his business when he retired?"

"No, he still liked to drop into the office now and then. He could never bring himself to give up his toys."

"Who's running the business now?"

"A man named David Unger. Dave's another one who'd been with Dad for a long time. Ten or twelve years, at least."

So Oliver Knowles had been a man who inspired loyalty . . . or else rewarded his employees so well that they had no desire to look for greener pastures. Marian wrote down *David Unger* in her notebook and asked for the address of the toy company's business offices. "Do you plan on selling the business?"

"God, I haven't even thought about that. I'll probably work out some sort of deal with Dave Unger. He has stock options, I know. The last few years that company's been as much his as Dad's anyway."

"I need to know who handled your father's legal affairs."

The ghost of a smile appeared on Knowles's face. "I was still a schoolboy back when Dad first needed a lawyer. He was just getting started in the toy business and didn't have much money, so he hired this kid fresh out of law school. Well, that 'kid' is in his sixties now . . . and still handling Dad's affairs."

Marian was amazed. "Your father held on to people, didn't he? He believed in commitments."

"That's exactly right, Lieutenant. Once he found people

he could trust, he trusted them completely. And to a man, they reciprocated. Dad was a good judge of people." Suddenly Knowles was on his feet, agitated. He started pacing. "That's how he became what he was—by knowing whom to trust, whom to avoid. The man had a gift for recognizing his own kind. He started with nothing. We were nothing. Dirt-poor Texas white trash. Dad was determined to get us out of that. And he did."

"Then you're from Texas? How long have you lived in New York?"

"Almost all my life. I barely remember Texas. I've never gone back."

"This sixty-year-old kid who handled your father's legal affairs—what's his name?"

"Elmore Zook. Isn't that a hell of a name? I called him Zookie the Cookie when I was a boy. I don't think he liked it, but he never said anything."

Elmore Zook, Marian's pen printed out. "Where's his office?"

"On Park . . . about Fifty-Seventh or so. Look, Lieutenant, I want to help, but I'm having trouble getting my head together. Too many feelings to sort out."

They always let you know when the interview was over. "Of course," Marian said, rising. "I'm sorry for your loss. I'll keep in touch."

"I'm counting on that," he said.

* 10 *

The stage doorkeeper waved her in. Marian walked silently to a place in the wings of the Broadhurst Theatre where she could see the stage without being in sight of the audience. The final scene of *The Apostrophe Thief* was just beginning; it was the only scene in the play in which the entire cast was onstage at the same time. Marian watched Kelly Ingram attempting to talk to the woman who played her mother, being ignored, feeling hurt, trying not to show it. *Showing* she was trying not to show it.

Kelly was doing that a lot more subtly than when the play first opened, Marian noticed. Kelly might claim to be getting the fidgets from having to say the same lines every night . . . but she was still working at it, still making a good performance even better. Kelly would scream with laughter if Marian ever told her she was a perfectionist; but in her own way, that's exactly what she was.

Marian thought she probably knew this scene by heart, she'd watched it so many times. She loved the play almost as much as she loved seeing her friend's success—almost, but not quite. Kelly's move from television glitter girl to legitimate actor had not been without its traumas, but she'd done it with the same style and grace and good humor that she did everything. Marian had no doubt that once the film version of the play was made, Kelly would be a movie star as well.

The play drew to its quiet, disturbing conclusion. There followed the usual stunned silence—and then the audience burst into applause. The performers were bowing, blowing kisses to the audience, flashing megawatt smiles . . . which disappeared the moment the curtains were closed. Kelly charged off the stage, smoke curling out of her ears. She stormed right past Marian without seeing her.

Her big, handsome leading man was thundering along right behind her. "Leo!" Ian Cavanaugh boomed. "Where the hell's Leo?"

Kelly swirled to face him; Ian ran into her, took a step back. Kelly thrust her face up into his. "Don't you ever, *ever* do that to me again!"

"If you could just bring yourself to pay attention once in a while," he growled, "you wouldn't get caught by surprise like that!"

"Meaning what?"

"Meaning I *told* you I was going to add new business tonight! Where's Leo?"

"You told me *nothing!*"

"I told you expressly that I was going to pick up a chair and carry it to the other side of the stage so you would have to adjust your exit accordingly. I even told you *which* chair I was going to move!"

"You're out of your skull!" Suddenly something penetrated and Kelly's head whipped around toward where Marian was standing. "Hi, toots." Back to her co-star. "Ian, you never said a word to me!"

He glanced over too. "Hello, Marian." Then he looked over Kelly's head and boomed out, "Will someone please get Leo Gunn?"

"What's Leo got to do with this?"

"Leo was standing right there when I told you. If you won't believe me, maybe you'll believe him."

She looked astonished. "Ian, you're making this up!"

"Making it up? Making it up?" He shifted into Shakespearean mode. "Mayhap the lady is calling me a speaker of untruths?" he boomed.

"I'm calling you *confused*, is what I'm calling you!"

The stage manager came hurrying up to them. "What's the problem?"

"Leo, will you please explain to this obstinate woman that I informed her well ahead of tonight's opening curtain that I was going to add some new stage business? Go ahead, tell her." The actor folded his arms across his chest, smiling smugly.

Leo's face was blank. "How do I know what you told her?"

Ian lost his smug look. "I told both of you at the same time!"

The stage manager shook his head. "You never told me at all," he said pointedly.

Ian was flabbergasted. "Damn! I was sure that was you who was standing there. I wonder who it was?"

Kelly threw up both arms in disgust and stomped away toward her dressing room, waving to Marian to follow. Leo Gunn was saying, "Ian, you surprised everybody—moving the chair like that. Kelly adjusted, but nobody knew it was coming."

In her dressing room, the play's leading lady plopped down in front of her make-up mirror while Marian closed the door. Kelly slathered cold cream all over her face and grabbed a tissue and started rubbing hard enough to take the skin off. "I am going to *kill* that man. I am going to strangle him with my own two lily-whites, chain his feet to an anvil, and toss him off the Triboro Bridge. That's what I'm going to do."

Marian stretched out on the daybed next to the make-up table. "He just forgot to tell you."

"He could have ruined the scene! You don't just spring something like that on people. But it's not only tonight. It's every night. Every night, Ian has to have something to complain about. Bitch, bitch, bitch. That's all he does anymore!"

"Hm. When's Abby getting back from California?"

"Oh, god . . . soon, I hope. Ian doesn't like going home to an empty house."

"Few men do."

"I talked to Abby a couple of days ago. She said she's spending most of her time waiting for meetings."

"I don't understand how that works," Marian said. "Why does the playwright have to go to script conferences? The play's already written."

Kelly wiped away the final traces of make-up and cold cream. "You don't think they're just going to film *The Apostrophe Thief* the way Abby wrote it, do you? Dear me, no. Then it would just be a filmed play, it wouldn't be a moooovie. No, they'll tweak a little here, cut a little there, 'open it out'— add stuff. Abby says it makes them feel creative."

"Abby permits this?"

"Abigail James is lucky to be allowed to sit in on the script conferences at all. 'In Hollywood, writers aren't worth the paper they write on'—quoth Abby. Let me get changed and we'll go grab a bite."

Marian picked up Kelly's copy of the *Times* and read an article about price-fixing while her friend changed into her street clothes. She finished the article and said, "What are you in the mood for tonight? French? Italian? Indian?"

"American," said Kelly. "Steak, preferably. Something I

can chew down on. That's what I'm in the mood for." She checked her appearance in the mirror. "I'm ready."

Marian didn't bother checking her own appearance. She'd stopped competing in the looks department years ago—the first time she took a good honest look at herself in the mirror. She'd made a choice no fourteen-year-old should ever have to make: should she spend time, energy, and money trying to change the way she looked, or should she stay the plainjane she was and live her life without the approval good-looking girls always garnered? It hadn't been an easy choice, but even then something had told her she'd avoid a lot of frustration by opting for the latter.

Before they could leave, there was a knock at the door. It was Ian Cavanaugh; he too had changed to street clothes. He was looking about as contrite as he ever managed to look.

"I'm sorry, Kelly," he said. "You were right. I only meant to tell you about the added stage business—I never actually got around to doing it. I apologize for being such an equine's derrière. Can you forgive me?"

"Sure, I can forgive you," Kelly said offhandedly, "until the next time it happens. You really ought to stop taking those grouchy pills."

He smiled sadly. "You mean I haven't been a barrel of laughs lately? Leo Gunn just gave me A Stern Talking-To, about what he called my constant complaining. I honestly hadn't realized I was being such a boor."

" 'Bear' is more like it," said his co-star.

"Leo said I owed every person in this company an apology. Have I really been that bad?"

"Oh yes," Kelly said cheerfully.

Ian cocked an eye in Marian's direction. "Have I done anything to you lately that I need to apologize for?"

She grinned. "Not a thing."

He sighed in mock relief and placed a hand on his chest. "Ah, someone left who doesn't hate me! I throw myself at your feet in gratitude!"

"Only metaphorically, I hope," Marian said. "Why don't you come with us? Get something to eat."

"Oh . . . no, I don't think so. I want to get home."

"Come along, Ian—it'll do you good," Kelly added. "Break your pattern a little. You always go straight home."

"I want to call Abby. I call her every night, after we're done. But have a good meal!" He tipped an imaginary hat to them and was gone.

Kelly locked the dressing room door behind her. "You know, he's why Leo Gunn banned visitors from coming backstage after the performance. Ian was offending too many people. He never does suffer fools gladly, even when he's not being a grouch."

Marian suddenly thought of Curt Holland—another who didn't suffer fools gladly. "I was wondering why there were no backstage visitors. This can't be helping the play."

"Oh, they're all outside in the cold, waiting by the stage door. Leo will lift the ban as soon as Ian gets over his grumps. As soon as Abby gets back. But brace yourself. You're going to have to elbow your way through the crowd."

The doorkeeper wished them both good night. Outside, the small crowd raised a cheer when they saw it was Kelly Ingram who was coming out. Kelly put on her celebrity smile—and then stopped cold.

"What's the matter?" Marian asked.

"She's here," Kelly said heavily.

* 11 *

The "she" turned out to be a mousy-haired woman in her mid-to-late twenties, wearing oversized glasses and a London Fog coat over leggings and lace-up boots—hardly the type to strike dread into the heart of so stalwart a soul as Kelly Ingram.

"Who is she?" Marian asked, low.

"Remember that fan I told you about?" Kelly muttered. "The one who never goes away? There she is."

The crowd surged forward, waving play programs and pens. Out-of-towners, Marian guessed, since the initial excitement of a new play drawing the New York crowd had passed. Kelly dutifully signed the programs thrust at her, chatting pleasantly with her fans.

But *the* fan, the one Kelly was not happy to see, waited until the autographing was done before making her move. She wriggled her way through the group still gathered around Kelly and gushed, "Oh, Kelly, you were just marvelous tonight! Just marvelous! One of your best performances ever!"

"Thank you," Kelly said coolly.

"But that new stage business of Ian Cavanaugh's—that part where he moves the chair? Do you know what I mean?"

Through clenched teeth, Kelly said, "Yes, Carla, I know what you mean."

"Well, that chair business distracts from your exit. He shouldn't be allowed to get away with that! I think you should speak to him about it."

"Thank you for sharing that." Kelly grabbed Marian's sleeve and headed toward the chauffeured limousine Kelly had waiting to pick her up every night. The driver was holding the door open for them.

"I mean it!" the fan insisted earnestly, trotting along beside Kelly. "He's upstaging you! Are you going to speak to him about it?"

"Carla, I can't talk to you now. We're on our way somewhere."

The fan glanced at Marian. "I don't believe I've met your friend."

"That's right," Kelly said blithely. "You haven't." She climbed into the limo, Marian right behind. The driver closed the door.

As the car pulled away, Kelly made a sound of frustration. "I am finding it increasingly difficult even to be civil to that girl! Woman, actually. But she acts like a girl."

"She seems harmless enough," Marian said. "Who is she?"

"Her name's Carla Banner and she is incurably stagestruck. Other than that, I don't really know anything about her. Except that she's always *there*. Every night she comes in with the crowd after intermission and looks for an empty seat. She's waiting at the stage door every night. She shows up at every public appearance I make. When I go out on a date, there's Carla hovering somewhere in the background, watching. Somehow she got hold of my phone number and leaves a message on my answering machine every day. *Every* day."

"She calls you by your first name."

Kelly sighed. "That's my fault. The first couple of times I met her, she just about Ms-Ingramed me to death. I told her to call me Kelly."

"Price of fame, kiddo."

"To hell with that. I am getting *very tired* of Carla Banner."

Kelly wanted steak, so they told the driver Gallagher's. Kelly created her usual stir when she made her entrance. Marian, trailing in her wake, got a kick out of the aplomb with which her friend carried it off. Neither of them objected when a table right in the middle of the room suddenly became available.

Kelly winked at Marian as they sat down. "Think everybody can see us here?"

"Hm. You could ask them to put the table up on a raised platform of some kind."

"I came in here one night with John Reddick and Abby and Ian," Kelly said, settling herself, "and they practically went out and hired an orchestra."

After they'd ordered, Marian asked, "How's John doing?"

"Hard to tell. He says the play's going to be a disaster— but he always says that."

John Reddick had directed *The Apostrophe Thief*, guiding Kelly skillfully through her first Broadway role. At present he was in England, directing the London production of the same play. He had not been invited to direct the film version.

Marian grinned. "Is he still madly, passionately in love with you?"

"He says so. Right before he starts complaining about how cold his flat is."

They were halfway through their steaks when Marian happened to glance over Kelly's shoulder and spotted a familiar figure at a table against the wall. "Guess who's here."

"Carla Banner," Kelly said without turning around. "I told you. She's everywhere."

Marian put down her fork. "You say this happens every time you go out?"

"Every time. You thought I was exaggerating, didn't you?"

"Did she follow us here?"

Kelly chewed a bite of steak, swallowed. "She must be independently wealthy or something. She spends a fortune on cabs. And she doesn't seem to have to be anyplace during the day. Yes, she followed us here."

Marian scowled. "Technically it's not invasion of privacy, because you're both in a public place. So far she's just being a pest, right? I doubt if you could get a restraining order. Those are usually issued only in cases of provable harassment."

Kelly nodded. "Thought it might be something like that. So far she hasn't found out where I live, thank god. Ian has had the same problem a number of times. He says the only way to put an end to it is to make them understand . . ." She hesitated. "Unequivocably?"

Marian had to think. "Unequivocally."

"Make them understand unequivocally that their attentions are not welcome. Ian advocates rudeness, name-calling, and yelling and screaming."

Marian smiled . . . but then thought of something. "Wait a minute. You said she doesn't know where you live—but she follows you everywhere?"

Kelly blanched. "She could have followed me home?"

"I'd bet on it. What makes you think she doesn't know?"

"Well, she's never come there, or left little notes with the super. She sends mail addressed to me at the theater."

"Nevertheless—"

"Oh shit. I have got to get rid of this person!"

Marian sympathized. "Have you ever tried telling her straight out?"

Kelly toyed with her wineglass. "That's what I'm going to have to do, isn't it? I suppose long-timers like Ian can handle this sort of thing without losing any sleep over it. But it's the first time it's ever happened to me."

"Here's your chance," Marian said with a grimace. "She's coming over."

Carla Banner approached their table diffidently, a please-like-me look on her puppy-dog face. "Hi again," she said softly. "I hope I'm not intruding, but—"

"You are," Kelly said shortly.

"But I wanted to urge you again to say something to Ian Cavanaugh about moving that chair," Carla went on, unhearing. "He really shouldn't be allowed to push you around like that."

"Sit down, Carla."

The young woman flushed with pleasure and sat quickly before Kelly could change her mind. "Oh, this is very nice of you, Kelly—"

"Now listen to me. Listen carefully. Ian Cavanaugh is not 'pushing me around.' And even if he were, that would be *my* business, not yours."

"Oh, but he—"

"I said listen to me. I want you to stop following me, Carla. I want you to stop calling me every day. I want you to stop showing up every place I go. Do you hear what I'm telling you? Get out of my life."

Carla laughed carelessly. "Oh, I couldn't stop going to *The Apostrophe Thief.* That's the high point of my—"

"Go to the play as often as you like," Kelly continued relentlessly, "but stop waiting by the stage door every night. Do you hear me? *Stop it.*"

The younger woman was still attempting to treat it all as a joke. "Hey, it's a free country!"

"I mean it, Carla." Once Kelly had made up her mind to

confront this irritant in her life, she wasn't pulling any punches. "You are invading my private space and I resent it. Have I made myself clear? I want you to stop. Find something else to do with yourself."

Marian thought: *At least she didn't say "Get a life."*

"But, Kelly," Carla said plaintively, "I'm your number-one fan! You don't know how important you are to—"

"Goodbye, Carla," Kelly interrupted. "Go away now. Don't come back."

Her face tightened. "You invited me to sit down." Pouting.

"And now I'm inviting you to stand up. And walk away. Far away. *Right now.*"

Carla Banner stood up slowly . . . and at the last minute thought of a face-saving out. "It's Ian Cavanaugh who's put you out of sorts. Don't worry, Kelly. What you just said—I won't hold it against you. I know you're upset." She hurried away before Kelly could answer.

Kelly growled. "I hate hit-and-run talkers."

Marian shook her head. "Your number-one fan seems to be hard of hearing."

"You don't think I got through to her?"

"I think she'll be back."

* 12 *

Snow had fallen during the night, not the city-prettifying snow but the kind that turned to slush one inch before it hit the sidewalks. Cold, wet, dark, dreary . . . happy February to you.

In muscle-flexing compensation for Out There, the stationhouse was defiantly overheated. Marian had put on tights under her trousers when the Weather Channel had told her what kind of day to expect. Tights and panties and trousers and tucked-in shirt and belt and jacket. Six layers around her middle; she was beginning to sweat. Marian slipped out of her jacket.

"Oliver Knowles's secretary," she said, "Lucas . . .?"

"Novak," O'Toole supplied.

"Lucas Novak. When's he getting back from Florida?"

"Today," Perlmutter said. "Plane gets in at ten-thirty. We'll catch him this afternoon. Mrs. R said he was down there for a family funeral."

"Mrs. R," Marian murmured. "The housekeeper. That's what Knowles's son calls her, Austin Knowles."

Perlmutter shrugged. "She said call her Mrs. R."

Ellen Rudolph, Marian reminded herself. "Two more I want you to check out." She handed Perlmutter a sheet of paper with two names and addresses on it. "You can split up on these. David Unger is the general manager of Oliver Knowles's toy company, and probably the next owner. Elmore Zook was Knowles's lawyer."

"I'll take the lawyer," Perlmutter said, tearing the page in half and giving Unger's name to O'Toole. "Beneficiaries, state of Knowles's finances . . . anything else?"

" 'The man had a gift for recognizing his own kind,' " Marian quoted.

"What say?" Perlmutter was copying both names into his notebook.

"It's something Austin Knowles said about his father. That he had a talent for finding people like himself. Try to get a personality fix on Unger and Zook. That should tell us a little of what Oliver Knowles was like."

"Son didn't tell you much?"

"As much as he could. His mother just died recently too . . . he's pretty shaken. What's the name of Knowles's toy company?"

O'Toole beamed. "O.K. Toys. Oliver Knowles. See? Initials."

"Got it, O'Toole," Marian said. "I want you to pin down the financial arrangement David Unger had with Knowles senior. The son said he has stock options."

Perlmutter looked up from his notebook. "Is he our suspect?"

"Not yet. But he's the only one so far with a possible motive. Pin down the money, O'Toole. Get the name of Unger's lawyer."

"Right."

She waved them out.

Marian spent the next hour reading reports. Sergeant Buchanan's squad seemed on top of their cases, but Sergeant Campos's detectives had two that had been dragging on too long. She stepped into the doorway of her office and saw Campos just sitting down at his desk in the squadroom.

"Sergeant Campos!" she called out. "In here, please." She must remember to stop saying *Please*.

Campos took an insultingly long time standing back up again. He moved toward Marian's office as if walking underwater. His face was carefully blank, but his body language spoke resentment in every movement.

Marian sat down at her desk and picked up the two reports. "The bar brawl that ended in a stabbing. You know the perp and you've got his address. Why haven't you picked him up?"

He was slow to answer. "DA's office says we need eyewitness testimony. To ID the perp."

"And?"

"We got two witnesses, but they're both outa town."

"Did you call them?"

One corner of his mouth lifted insolently. "Of course I called 'em."

"And? Come on, Campos, don't make me drag it out of you."

"They'll be back, one of 'em tonight. We'll get the ID tomorrow and wrap it up then."

"All right." She put that report aside. "What about the Sanderson case?"

The sergeant's manner shifted slightly . . . more defensive now? "We got nothin' that proves Sanderson's a fence. The guy runs a clean shop, far as we can tell."

Marian sat back in her chair. "There's nothing in the report about a tail."

"Oh hell, I'd have to pull men off bigger cases to give 'im a round-the-clock. It's not worth it, just to nab one more penny-ante fence. You know that . . . *Lieutenant*."

She overlooked his tone and asked, "How do you know he's penny-ante?"

"Hey, stands to reason, don't it? Have you seen his shop? Hanging by a thread."

"Have you seen his home?"

Campos didn't answer.

"How well does he live, Campos? What does he drive? Where does he have his suits made? The one time he was in here, that was no off-the-rack he was wearing. The man has money, Campos. Where does it come from?"

Campos muttered something unintelligible.

"The truth is," Marian went on, "you don't know anything about this guy." She looked at the report. "Detectives Walker and Dowd, acting on a complaint from another small businessman in the building, visited Sanderson, looked around, didn't see anything wrong, brought Sanderson in for questioning once, and then let it drop." She raised her eyes to Campos. "No follow-up. None."

The sergeant clenched his jaw. "I'm tellin' you, this is penny-ante stuff."

"I sincerely hope you're right. But you don't know it and I don't know it. Walker and Dowd sure as hell don't know it. It's sloppy police work, Campos."

He let his anger show. "You tellin' me how to do my job?"

"Yes." She stared at him. "You know better than to let Walker and Dowd get away with that. Have they been lying down on the job?"

"No." He was very firm about that. "They're two of my best detectives."

At least he's protective of his men; that's good. "Then go light a fire under them. Get this taken care of."

"Oh yes, *ma'am*, Lieutenant, *ma'am*." He turned to go.

"Sergeant!" He stopped. "Close the door."

It took him forever, but he closed the door.

Marian stood up and asked, "Do you have a problem

working for me, Campos?" When he didn't say anything, she snapped, "I expect an answer when I ask a question."

"I don't have a problem . . . *ma'am*." He was dangerously close to sneering.

"I think you do. And I think you're having trouble remembering that it's *your* problem. Because I'm not going to walk out of this job just to make you happy, Campos. Did you get that? I'm not. Ever. Going. To go. Away." She took a breath. "Accept it, and adjust. And do it fast, will you? I don't have time for this horseshit." She walked over and opened the door. "Go on."

She stood in the doorway watching him make his way back to his desk, a lot more rapidly than he'd left it. He was going to have to learn to take orders from a woman or transfer out. Marian had no intention of putting up with his sulks.

At the nearest desk, Detective Dowd was on the phone. "Call for you, Lieutenant—line one. Guy named Holland."

She went back to her phone and pressed the button. "Holland?"

"I've come across something rather interesting in our search for the mysterious Laura Cisney," he said without preamble. "I can show you on the computer better than I can tell you. Do you have time to come here?"

"I'll be there in twenty minutes," she said, and hung up.

* 13 *

The only other time Marian had seen Curt Holland's suite of offices, it had been brand-new and bare of furnishings; now it looked like a flight control center at NASA. Holland was one of the ever-increasing new breed of private investigators, the computer detective. "Don't even mention a trench coat in my presence," he'd once snarled. Yet he still saw a need to keep street operatives such as Zoe Esterhaus on his payroll.

Marian didn't have to ring for admittance. A scanning camera mounted outside the office had picked her up as she walked down the hall corridor; the door buzzed open and Holland was waiting inside. "Come look at my table," he said with a smug smile.

"Table?" Marian slipped out of her coat and folded it over one arm. She glanced down a hallway where two men, talking loudly in Computerspeak, left one office and went into another.

Holland led her inside the reception area. A woman wearing a prim pearl-gray dress with a white collar and seated behind the one desk there gave Marian a frank looking-over, this woman for whom her boss had stood waiting by the door. Holland pointed to a small leather-topped writing table. "We keep that for clients to use when signing contracts and writing checks and the like. André says that the mysterious Laura Cisney wrote her phony name on our agreement form while sitting right there. Mrs. Grainger," he nodded toward the receptionist, "says no one else used the table that day."

Marian's eyes widened. "Prints."

He nodded. "Almost a full set."

André Flood walked by, carrying an armload of printouts. "Hello, Lieutenant Larch." He disappeared into an office down the hallway.

Holland's eyebrows shot up. "Well. You must have created quite an impression, if André remembers you after only one meeting."

"I don't see how," Marian said. "He never once looked at me during the entire interview."

"That's our André. Let's go to my office." Holland led the way.

Inside the office, Holland took her coat and hung it in a closet. "I looked in AFIS," he said—and laughed at Marian's expression. A former agent, Holland knew his way around the FBI's computer set-up, including its Automated Fingerprint Identification System. And he never seemed to have any trouble getting through its constantly changing security.

Marian sighed. "What did you find?"

"What do you want? Name? Age? Address?"

"Holland!"

"None of which will do you the least bit of good," he added blandly. "Her name is Rosalind Bowman, for all the help that's going to be, and she's forty-five years old." He stepped over to a small conference table and picked up a folder. "Here's what we found."

"Rosalind Bowman," Marian repeated as she opened the folder. "Why was she in AFIS? She must have a record."

"Bowman was a political activist back in the sixties. She

took part in a sit-in demonstration against a Midwest university holding government contracts for chemical research, and along with a hundred others she refused a police order to vacate the premises. Rosalind Bowman spent one night in jail, and now Big Brother has her prints on file forevermore."

"That's all she did?" Marian was skimming through the file, impressed at how much Holland had learned about Bowman in so short a time.

"That's all. She's led a completely ordinary life until recently. Came to New York after college, worked as a newswriter for local radio and television, worked her way up to producer-writer on features, all on the local level. Got married. No children. Stopped working to stay home and care for her husband, who'd had a stroke. Widowed last year."

"So what happened recently?"

"She dropped out of sight," Holland said. "Deliberately. That's what I want you to see. Sit here." He pulled a chair in front of a computer.

Marian sat, acutely aware of the hand he dropped casually on her shoulder as he stood behind her. "What am I looking at?"

"Bowman's bank accounts." There were three open on the screen. "One checking, two savings. She cleaned them out. Notice the dates."

"All the same day."

"Now look at this." He tapped out a command with his right hand and another window opened on the screen. "She closed her Con Edison account the next day. And these." More windows.

His hand was burning a place on her left shoulder. "Closed all her other utility accounts, canceled phone and cable," Marian read from the screen. All within, what—three or four days?"

"It took her five days altogether . . . department store accounts and the like." Holland reached around her and used both hands on the keyboard. The screen cleared and a new set of windows appeared. "Credit card accounts. She closed every one of them."

Marian frowned. "She wouldn't cancel credit cards if she was just moving away, leaving town."

He called up a new screen. "Havery Van and Storage. Bowman paid their minimum three months' storage fee but made no arrangement for her household goods to be shipped to another city. What do you want to bet that's the last Havery Van and Storage ever hears of Rosalind Bowman?"

"She's just abandoning everything?" At the back of her mind, a thought was born: *He could have told me all this over the phone.*

Holland had both hands on her shoulders now. "This morning I sent Zoe Esterhaus over to talk to Bowman's neighbors. She found one neighbor who'd been especially friendly with our missing lady. The neighbor says Bowman moved back to her hometown—Lansing, Michigan. The last she saw of Bowman, she was waving goodbye from the back-seat of a cab."

"No forwarding address."

"Right. Bowman said she'd be staying with relatives until she found a place and then she'd write. But she won't."

Marian stood up to escape from those hands. "You checked airlines."

"Right before I called you. No Rosalind Bowman or Laura Cisney on any flights to Lansing. Or to anyplace else. But we already know she never left New York. She was here in this office on Friday."

"As Laura Cisney."

"Probably a name she concocted in the elevator on the

way up. If she has another identity established, it won't be in the name of Laura Cisney. No, she's been too thorough to reveal her new identity that casually." Holland smiled wryly. "What she's done has been to commit an act of symbolic suicide. She's killed off Rosalind Bowman and written *finis* to the life that Rosalind Bowman lived. It's as if she'd died."

"The lady doesn't want to be found," Marian said with a nod. "But why hang around here if she wants to start a new life elsewhere?"

Holland cocked an eyebrow. "Perhaps the lady had one more account to close before she left," he suggested.

Marian nodded. "Oliver Knowles. Did you find any connection between the two of them?"

"Not even a trace of one. And believe me, we looked."

Marian believed him. "Yet somehow Knowles had a big enough impact on her that she abandoned everything and everyone she knew in her life . . . and hired your agency to follow him before she made her final escape. What do you suppose she wanted to do? She wouldn't have had him followed if she'd already hired a hit man."

Holland agreed. "But whatever she had in mind, she's probably gone now—now that Knowles is dead."

"I suspect you're right. Anyway, this does tell us that Knowles was not the simple toymaker he appeared to be." She picked up the folder containing the information Holland had gathered about Rosalind Bowman. "May I take this?"

"Of course." A sardonic smile. "Well, Lieutenant, am I now off the hook with the NYPD?"

"Oh, Holland, you were never on the hook," she said with a laugh. "I'm grateful for all your help. Thank you."

He got a glint in his eye. "So, are you willing to admit there are things a private agency can do that the police can't?"

There it was: the sore spot that never quite healed. "I've always admitted that," she said mildly.

"Yet you chose to stay with the police rather than work with me," Holland said tightly. "Saint Murtaugh dangles a lieutenancy in front of your nose and you go for it without a second thought."

"Of course I went for it," Marian said a little less mildly. "It's what I've worked toward all my adult life. I never told you I'd join your agency."

"No, you never did. I offered you *anything you wanted*—and you turned me down."

"And you're never going to let me forget it, are you?"

He was silent a moment, and then said softly: "You betrayed me, Marian."

"*What?*" She was astounded. "I *betrayed* you?"

"I thought I had finally found one person on this earth I could trust," he said. "But you turned away from me at the moment I needed you the most."

Marian was furious. "Needed me? God, you can be so melodramatic! All I did was choose one job over another job. Only *you* would turn that into a personal betrayal!"

"What was I to think? You turned your back on me."

"Oh, Holland," she said with a sigh. "I never turned my back on you. It was you who shut me out." They stared at each other wordlessly a moment, and then Marian said, "Look, this isn't getting us anywhere. And I've got to get going. Where'd you put my coat?"

He took his time about going to the closet door and sliding her coat off the hanger. He opened his mouth to speak, but then shut it again. He brought her the coat and held it as she slipped into it . . . and then shot both arms around her from the back.

Marian gave in to a rush of pleasure. *God, he felt good!*

She relished the feel of him, his weight against her back, his cheek pressed against hers, his arms circling her like iron clamps. With an effort she got him to loosen his grip enough for her to turn to face him. And then they were locked tightly together, as if trying to get inside each other; they couldn't stand that way long before it began to affect them physically. He even tasted good.

When they came up for air, Marian realized she had her hands bunched into fists pressing against his back. She forced herself to relax and took a step away, examining his face. He looked as tense as she felt. She gave a self-deprecating laugh and said, "Whew. I thought we were done with that, but I guess we're not."

"Not by a long shot," he agreed, wiping the palms of his hands on his trousers legs. "We've wasted a lot of time, you and I."

Yes, you have. "Well, I'm willing to do some catching up . . . in case I didn't make that clear just now."

He laughed and reached for her.

This time they almost ended up on the conference table. But Marian-on-duty was still Marian on duty. "No time, no time," she moaned. "I'm supposed to be investigating a murder, remember? I think I'd better wash my face."

Holland went with her into his private restroom. He watched her reflection as she washed and applied lipstick, the only make-up she wore . . . when she remembered it. "We're linked, you know," Holland said quietly.

"I know."

"Whether you like the idea or not, we need each other."

"Oh my, don't say that." She dropped the lipstick into her bag and made eye contact with him in the mirror. "Promise me one thing, Holland. Promise me you'll never say 'I need you.' "

He looked surprised. "All right. But tell me why."

Marian sighed. "Because more women have been trapped by those three little words than by 'I love you.' " She edged past him, back into the office. "Let's not need each other," she said. "Let's just, well, choose each other."

"Ah, a linkage forged by preference rather than by necessity . . . I see. Does that make a stronger chain?"

"I think so. But we'll have to finish this image-making some other time. I really must go."

He led her back to the office's outside entrance. "Dinner tonight?" he asked. At the reception desk, Mrs. Grainger's head snapped around.

"Not tonight," Marian said regretfully. "My former partner is taking me to meet his future mother-in-law."

"Malecki? Ivan Malecki's getting married?"

"Yep." She hesitated. "I'm going to be his best man."

His eyebrows rose. "Best . . . *man?*"

"Holland," she warned.

He swallowed his laugh and raised both hands, palms outward. He was still standing that way when she left.

* 14 *

Marian stopped at a quick-service lunch counter on her way back, but she was only half-finished when her beeper sounded. She used the pay phone on the wall to call in. It was Campos, telling her he'd put a tail on the man suspected of being a fence. He'd waited until lunchtime to disturb her with that bit of nonessential news.

"Shithead," she said out loud as she sat back down at the counter; the two men on either side studiously ignored her. Marian finished her lunch in a hurry and then set her empty coffee cup down so hard she broke the handle off; the counterman told her she'd have to pay for it. With a long-suffering sigh, Marian paid up and left. The weather outside was so miserable she was glad of the tights under her trousers. The wind blowing in her face was wet and cold, but the next wave of slushy snow was holding off.

Back in her roasting office, Marian yelled for someone to call Maintenance about the heat. She checked her messages; long one from Perlmutter, but no word from O'Toole. Perlmutter's visit to Elmore Zook, Oliver Knowles's lawyer, had resulted in no surprises. Trust funds for housekeeper Ellen Rudolph and secretary Lucas Novak, as Austin Knowles had said. A generous gift to the ASPCA and another to a local animal-rescue group. Everything else went to the son, Austin Knowles. David Unger had an option to buy additional shares of O.K. Toys. Zook had said that Austin Knowles was offering to sell a majority of the shares to Unger, more than the will required him to dispose of. Perlmutter left word that he was going to grab a bite and then come in.

Feeling fidgety, Marian stood up and stretched. The only personal item Oliver Knowles had carried in his billfold was a photo of a cat, and he'd left bequests for two animal-protection organizations. So he liked kitties and he made toys for children. Santa Claus.

Then why did someone arrange his murder? And what threat did he pose to Rosalind Bowman that she should go to such desperate lengths to make herself untraceable? And having done so, why didn't she just go? What was that last "account" she wanted to settle before she left New York? There had to be money involved in this—not the inheritance, that seemed aboveboard. What kind of records did that toy company keep? If Holland could get into the O.K. Toys computers—

Whoa.

Had she really thought that? *If Holland could get into the O.K. Toys computers* . . . good god. She'd actually thought of asking him to do one of his illegal snooping jobs? She'd been trying not to think about Holland at all. But it was hard not to think about Holland. It was *very* hard not to think about him. Well, impossible, actually. She'd been doing pretty well at pushing him out of her head for the last month, until the Oliver Knowles killing brought him back into her life. But now he *was* back, oh yes, just as intrusively as ever. The truth was, her encounter with Holland that morning had left her with an unscratched itch and she wasn't in the best of moods.

So when Detective O'Toole came barging in, she almost bit his head off. "*What?*" she roared.

He took a step back. "Report on David Unger and O.K. Toys."

"I told you to call in."

"Yeah, Lieutenant, but I got something here you'll want to see."

Marian counted to ten and sat at her desk. "Show me." O'Toole placed on O.K. Toys catalog in front of her. "A toy catalog."

"That's their current catalog. Look at the date. Inside front cover, small print at the bottom."

She looked where he said. "It's four years old."

O'Toole was nodding. "Toy companies put out several catalogs each year. They have to, to compete. But O.K. Toys doesn't bother. Don't you find that interesting?"

Marian nodded. "Very interesting. Where's their factory?"

He pulled up a chair and sat down. "They don't have one. Not anymore. They stopped manufacturing a few years ago, David Unger says, and sold the last factory in New Jersey. Now they buy from vendors and resell, catalog sales exclusively. Except that their catalog is four years old."

"Did Unger say this was their latest printed?"

"I asked for a current catalog and that's what he handed me. Took it off of a stack."

"Money."

"Unger says he already owns ten percent of O.K. Toys. Knowles had shown him his will, he says, and that gave him an option to buy another thirty-five percent. But Unger says Austin Knowles, the son, is going to sell him more than that. Enough to make him the majority stockholder."

"That part's true," Marian said. "Austin Knowles told me that himself, and Elmore Zook confirmed it this morning. Who's Unger's lawyer?"

O'Toole grinned. "Elmore Zook."

Just then Perlmutter appeared in the doorway, back from lunch. "Something at O.K. Toys?"

"Fill him in, O'Toole," Marian said.

Perlmutter took the only other chair as O'Toole repeated what he'd just said. "Interesting," Perlmutter commented when his partner had finished. "Austin Knowles and David Unger using the same lawyer. You'd think Unger would want separate representation. But if it's a friendly sale and Zook is the business's lawyer, I guess it makes sense."

"There's something else." O'Toole scratched the back of his neck. "No toys on display in that office. No pictures of toys on the walls. Whether they're manufacturing or just distributing, they oughta have some toys around. That office coulda been selling jock straps, for all I could tell. Wasn't right."

Marian pursed her lips. "You have kids, O'Toole?"

"Yeah, two. And we get toy catalogs in the mail all the time. O.K. Toys just doesn't smell right, Lieutenant."

The man had a gift for recognizing his own kind, Austin Knowles had said. "Tell me about the two men. Zook and Unger."

Perlmutter and O'Toole could have been talking about the same man. Courteous, well-spoken, educated, cooperative without volunteering anything. Efficient; spoke straight to the point without wasting time or words. Poised. Relaxed. The only differences between the lawyer and the toy company manager were physical ones. Zook was in his sixties, Unger was about forty; Zook was stout, Unger was not; Zook was partially bald, Unger could do with a haircut, in O'Toole's opinion. And both detectives agreed that what they'd seen had been a façade, a mask worn for talking to the police.

"There may be nothing in that," Marian pointed out. "Most professional people have a persona they put on when dealing with the public. So, O'Toole, what do you think is going on at O.K. Toys?"

He shrugged. "A money-laundering operation? They've got a good set-up for it. Let me tell you what I did. I called the IRS and told them I thought O.K. Toys was cooking its books."

"You *what?*" Marian and Perlmutter yelled at the same time.

O'Toole blanched. "I thought we could get the IRS to do some of our work for us—check them out, like."

"O'Toole, that is the dumbest thing I have heard since . . . since I don't remember when," Marian said angrily. "The DA's office has accountants—you don't use the IRS for something like that. You don't *use* the IRS for anything. Once Internal Revenue gets its hooks into those books, we'll *never* get a look at them. You may have just ended this investigation right here."

The rookie detective looked stricken. "Oh jeez, I didn't think of—"

"No, you didn't think, did you? O'Toole, do you remember standing right here in this office and listening to me tell you not to do *anything* without checking with Perlmutter first? Do you remember that? Do you?"

He gulped. "Yes."

"You damned well had better remember it from now on. Now you go get on that phone and call the IRS and tell them you made a biiiig mistake, that the toy company is on the up-and-up and there's no need for the IRS to investigate."

"I talked to three people there."

"Then call all three of them. Then find out if they talked to anyone else there and call *them*. You don't do anything else with your life until you squash this—do you understand? Now *move*."

Red-faced, O'Toole hurried out to his desk to start phoning.

Perlmutter cocked an eyebrow at Marian. "Kind of rough on him, weren't you, Lieutenant?"

"I'm always rough on people who don't know how to listen," she replied shortly. "Come on. Let's go talk to Lucas Novak."

* 15 *

One look at Oliver Knowles's Central Park South apartment told Marian more about the dead man than anything the investigation had turned up so far. The man had had sybaritic tastes . . . and the wherewithal to indulge them.

"A lot of money in toys, huh?" Perlmutter had murmured when they first went in.

It was the trains that got to Marian. The luxurious furnishings, some of which must be antiques, were impressive in their own right. But the most elaborate train set Marian had ever seen took up two entire rooms in a building standing on some of the highest-priced real estate in the world. Oliver Knowles was not a man to deny himself what he wanted.

Ellen Rudolph, the late-fiftyish or early-sixtyish housekeeper, was having trouble keeping back her tears. "Mr. Knowles loved those trains," she said as she showed the detectives around. "After he retired, he'd spend hours in there. Always building, changing the layout, trying new switching systems and the like." She smiled sadly. "Lucas and I learned a lot about trains, living here."

"Where is Lucas Novak?" Perlmutter wanted to know.

"He said he'd be right back. He had an errand to run."

"How long have you lived here, Mrs. Rudolph?" Marian asked.

"Call me Mrs. R," the housekeeper said. "Everyone does. I've been looking after Mr. Knowles for twenty-one years. I came to work for him right after my husband died, and I've been with him ever since. Was with him," she amended. She took a tissue out of a pocket and blew her nose. "Excuse me. I'm just getting over the flu."

"That's a long time to work for one man," Marian said. "What's going to happen to the trains?"

Mrs. R's face took on a pinched, disapproving look. "Austin is going to auction them off. He's going to auction off the entire contents of the apartment. The appraiser is coming tomorrow." She shook her head. "How can he do that? How can he just auction off his father's things?"

Perlmutter spoke up. "Who's going to take the cat?"

The housekeeper looked blank. "What cat?"

"Mr. Knowles had a photo of a cat in his billfold."

"Oh, that must be Phineas. White Persian? Phineas died four or five years ago. Mr. Knowles never got another cat."

Marian said, "May we see the bedroom, Mrs. R?"

"Certainly." She led the way.

Perlmutter said to Marian, low, "The guy carried a photo of a dead cat but no pictures of his wife or son?"

Knowles's bedroom was solidly masculine in a traditional way—heavy furniture, muted colors, no ruffles or flounces. Marian slid open the door of the large walk-in closet: all men's clothing. "Did Mrs. Knowles have a separate bedroom?"

Mrs. R looked shocked. "Oh, Mrs. Knowles never lived here! Didn't you know, Lieutenant? They'd been separated—oh, it must be thirty years."

Marian shot a look at Perlmutter, who shrugged. "No, we didn't know. No divorce?"

"No. Mr. Knowles supported her and put Austin through college, but they were never divorced."

They started back toward the living room. Marian asked, "Did Austin live with his mother?"

The housekeeper said he did. "Austin was just a schoolboy when they separated, and it was hard on him. Still, he was over here a lot. Mrs. Knowles didn't like that."

"Why not?"

Mrs. R just shook her head. "Some women are so vindictive. She didn't want Austin to have anything to do with his father. Sometimes Austin would be so upset when he came here—after a row with his mother, I mean." At that moment they heard the door in the apartment entryway open. "There's Lucas now," the housekeeper said, and went to meet him.

Marian could hear the murmur of their voices from the vicinity of the front door. Mrs. R returned, followed by a middle-aged man whose expensive suit didn't quite hide the fact that he was going to fat. He peered at Perlmutter querulously through rimless spectacles.

Mrs. R said, "Lucas, this is Lieutenant Larch and Detective . . . ?"

"Perlmutter," he supplied.

Lucas Novak shifted his gaze to Marian. "You're the lieutenant?"

"I'm the lieutenant," she said neutrally. "Could we sit down? We need to ask you a few things."

"Of course. But I don't know what I can tell you."

They found seats, all but Mrs. R who said, "I'll fix some tea. Or would you prefer coffee, Lieutenant?"

"Nothing for me, thanks." Perlmutter declined as well.

As soon as the housekeeper had left, Novak said, "Do you have a line on the man who shot Oliver?"

"He was a hired killer, Mr. Novak," Marian said. "We're trying to find out who hired him. And why."

"Yes, why?" He frowned. "There's no reason. None. He must have killed the wrong man. That's the only explanation."

Perlmutter cleared his throat. "Professionals don't make that kind of mistake. The hitter followed him onto a crowded bus, shot him, and got off before anyone knew what had happened. Cool and sure. There was no mistake."

"Mr. Novak," Marian said, "why did a retired toymaker need a secretary? What did you do for him, exactly?"

"Not so much as before," Novak said. "Oliver still maintained an interest in the business, although he was no longer involved in the day-to-day running of it. Mostly what I've been doing the last couple of years is tending to his personal affairs—correspondence, taxes, bill-paying. That's what I've always done."

"You handled his personal correspondence? Anything out of the ordinary there lately?"

Novak slowly shook his head. "There wasn't much of it. Primarily Oliver liked to keep in touch with business contacts he'd made over the years."

"Was he in touch with anyone in Texas?"

The secretary looked surprised. "No, no one. Why do you ask that?"

"He was from Texas, wasn't he?"

"Yes, but he'd cut all ties with that early life—long before I came to work for him."

"And you saw *all* his correspondence?"

"Every piece. When the mail was delivered, I saw it before he did. I threw out the advertisements and solicitation letters, that sort of thing, and passed on to him only those letters I knew he'd be interested in seeing."

So Novak had screened Knowles's mail. Perhaps keeping something from him? "No threatening letters?"

He gave her the ghost of a smile. "No, Lieutenant."

Marian sat back in her chair; Perlmutter picked up his cue and asked, "You've been in Florida?"

"Attending a funeral," Novak said. "My uncle's. He'd raised me . . . my parents were killed in a traffic accident when I was ten. I'd planned to stay on another few days until Mrs. R called and told me Oliver had been shot."

All the time he was talking, Marian was studying him. He was very composed for someone who'd just lost two older men to whom he'd been close. As if reading her mind, Perlmutter asked, "What are you going to do now?"

"I haven't decided yet. Oliver left me an annuity, I know. But I've had a standing offer for years from one of Oliver's associates to come work for him. They used to joke about it—Oliver's leaving me to the associate in his will, that sort of thing."

"Who is this associate?" Marian wanted to know.

"Oliver's lawyer. His name is Elmore Zook."

All in the family, Marian thought. She listened as Perlmutter went on probing, trying to find some hint of a reason anyone would want Knowles dead. But Novak had nothing at all to tell them.

Abruptly, she asked, "What do you think of David Unger?"

"A good man," Novak answered without hesitation. "Oliver trusted him." He said the last as if that were the unquestioned standard by which all people were to be judged.

Soon after that, Mrs. R brought Novak a cup of tea. Marian thanked them for their help, which was perhaps more than they realized; she and Perlmutter left.

Perlmutter was driving. "Whaddaya think, Lieutenant?"

"I think Oliver Knowles was a genius at surrounding himself with people on whose loyalty he could rely. Look at the way the housekeeper automatically sided with him in his quarrel with his wife."

"Huh. She knew which side her bread was buttered on."

"It's more than that." Marian thought back. "She called Mrs. Knowles vindictive. Too bad the lady isn't still with us to tell her side of the story. Perlmutter, tomorrow I want you to go see Austin Knowles. Find out what the trouble was between his parents."

He looked surprised. "You think that's pertinent?"

"Probably not. But so far the late Mrs. Knowles is the only one we've come across who didn't think the late Mr. Knowles was a saint."

When they were back in the stationhouse, Marian went looking for Captain Murtaugh. She found him leaning against the wall by the coffee machine, staring dourly at the brown liquid in the paper cup he was holding.

"Why do they call this coffee?" he greeted her glumly. "It doesn't even remotely resemble the real stuff."

"The hot chocolate's not bad," she said.

"But it doesn't have caffeine," the captain objected. He took a swallow and made a face. "The Knowles case? Do you have a suspect?"

"A potential. I'm going to talk to him tomorrow. David Unger, the manager and soon-to-be majority stockholder of O.K. Toys. He's the only one who will be noticeably better off because of Knowles's death, but we still have no link between him and the shooter. Could we get a DA's accountant to go over the company books?"

Murtaugh nodded once. "I'll get the warrant. Anything else?"

"Tell him to look for recent transactions. Lists of vendors and customers for the past year."

The captain suddenly looked interested. "Not really a toy business?"

"O'Toole thinks there's something fishy there. Should be easy to prove, one way or the other."

"What are you going to do? Call the vendors and verify recorded orders?"

"That's the idea. We shouldn't have to call them all."

Murtaugh looked at her, hard. "Gut response, Larch. What do you think was going on?"

She took a breath. "I think Oliver Knowles went to extraordinary lengths to insulate himself. He built up a whole network of bought-and-paid-for loyalty which turned out to be extraordinarily reliable. The man was a shrewd judge of people, Captain. But he must have made one mistake, one lapse in judgement. And that one mistake cost him his life."

"Someone close to him, then? You've ruled out business competitors?"

"He was out of business. Retired. A competitor would have gone after him when he was still a player."

The captain nodded. "Let me know what you learn about Unger."

Marian said she would and turned to go—and then turned back. "Captain, you remember the wedding I'm going to be in?"

His face broke into a grin. "Best man."

"I'm following your advice. Tonight I'm meeting the bride's mother."

"She'll fill you in, count on it. Have fun."

"Fun?" She shuddered. "I'm dreading it."

Marian left him still leaning by the coffee machine. As

she passed Dowd's desk, he said without looking up: "Package on your desk. Messenger brought it."

"Thanks, Dowd."

It was an ordinary mailing bag. She found the tab on the back and ripped the bag open.

Inside was a set of keys to Holland's apartment.

* 16 *

"The thing to remember," Ivan Malecki said, "is always to agree with her. The lady has very pronounced opinions. Got that?"

"Mm," said Marian.

"I mean about everything, Marian. If she tells you the world is flat, you nod knowingly and say you'd always suspected that was true."

"How does she feel about your asking me to be your best man?"

Ivan laughed out loud. "First time I've ever seen her not know what to think. When I told her my former partner was going to be my best man, she was pleased—that demonstrated loyalty on my part, ya see. But when I said my former partner is a woman, she hit the ceiling. It was outrageous, she never heard of such a thing, was I trying to insult her daughter, et goddam cetera." He laughed again. "*Then* I told her you were a police lieutenant—and she just stood there with her mouth working, not knowing what to say. God, I loved it."

"Oh boy."

"So she's torn between your rank and your, er, womanness. Just come on like an authority figure and you'll be okay."

Marian groaned.

Ivan pulled up to the curb. "Here we are." They were in a section of Queens that Marian didn't know, a neighborhood of free-standing houses squeezed close together on narrow lots. The Yelincic house—their destination—had the porch light on. They were expected.

Claire Yelincic opened the door, a pretty blond past the flush of girlhood but with an open smile and straight gaze that had made Marian like her from the first time they met. Claire gave Ivan a quick kiss and turned to Marian. "She'll swoop in on you like a hawk, Marian—brace yourself."

"Hanh," Marian said weakly.

"Believe it or not, she's a little nervous about meeting you. And I apologize in advance for all the personal questions she'll ask."

"Claire! You don't have to do that."

Ivan and Claire were nodding in unison. "Yes, she does," the former said.

"Come on in," Claire told them.

They stepped into a hallway that ran straight back, doorways to the right and left and a stairway about halfway down the hall. Claire no longer lived with her parents, but this was the house she'd grown up in. She hung up Marian's and Ivan's coats and led them through the doorway to the left into the living room.

Marian had built up a picture in her mind of a stout, matronly woman in a flowered dress. But Mrs. Yelincic was thin and wiry and wore a navy blue polyester pantsuit. She stood in front of an artificial fireplace with her hands folded neatly at her waist, like a contralto in the church choir waiting for her solo. Marian caught a movement out of the corner of her eye and turned to see a gray, featureless man rising from a rocking chair, a newspaper in one hand.

Claire did the honors, introducing her as Lieutenant

Larch, no first name. Mrs. Yelincic advanced to meet her, one claw extended; Marian gave both parents what she hoped was an authoritative handshake. "We are honored to meet you, Lieutenant," Mrs. Yelincic said in a voice like razor blades. Mr. Yelincic smiled and nodded.

Marian summoned her you-have-the-right-to-remain-silent voice and said, "It's very gracious of you to help me out, Mrs. Yelincic. I want to make sure that everything is done right."

"Yes, I certainly hope so." Mrs. Yelincic smiled an artificial smile. "But first, let's go into the dining room. We waited to have dessert with you."

"Thank you, Ivan and I stopped for a bite on the way over . . ." Behind his future mother-in-law, Ivan was vigorously nodding his head. ". . . but we didn't have dessert," Marian finished with an attempt at enthusiasm.

"Today I have baked a torte," Mrs. Yelincic confided. "You must tell me what you think."

So they were to go through an eating ritual first, before they could get down to business. They all trooped across the hall to the dining room, where Marian sat down to her second dessert of the evening. She didn't have to lie when she told their hostess the torte was delicious.

"I don't put raisins or any kind of fruit in the thin layers," Mrs. Yelincic announced. "That's wrong. I don't care how many recipes call for dried dates or figs or anything else. Fruit does not belong in a torte. Nuts, yes. But no fruit."

Ivan and Claire quickly agreed; Marian followed suit. Mr. Yelincic nodded and smiled.

"Do you cook, Lieutenant?" Razor-blades voice, trying to sound innocent.

Marian saw the trap. "I'm a weekend-only cook now, I'm afraid. That's one of the things I've hated having to give up. I wish I still had the time to spend in the kitchen that real cooking demands. Don't you just hate those quickie meals tossed together at the last minute?"

Mrs. Yelincic heartily agreed. "Push something in the microwave, eat five minutes later—that's not cooking." Ivan was trying not to laugh.

Claire said, "Mama, you work all day, sometimes you're just too tired to cook when you get home."

"Cook on weekends. Freeze. Then you have a good dinner waiting for you every night."

"Oh, Mama." Claire glanced at Ivan mischievously. "I suppose we could spend our weekends cooking." Ivan put on an angelic look.

But Marian had passed the first test; time for the second. "But Lieutenant," Razor Blades went on, "doesn't it bother you, working with all those men?"

Marian pretended to think it over. "I have two women detectives working under me—all the rest are men. But you know, I never stop to think whether I'm giving instructions to a man or a woman. I work with professionals. That's all that matters." Stressing her authority—*working under me* and *giving instructions.*

"But don't you get embarrassed?" the woman persisted. "Changing clothes in the same locker room!" She was clearly scandalized.

"Oh, we have separate locker rooms. That's never been an issue."

Mrs. Yelincic looked unbelieving. "I heard all the police changed and showered together."

Oh dear. "Why don't you come to Midtown South for a visit someday? I'll show you the women's locker room. It's not pretty, but it is off-limits to the men." It was, in fact, an ordinary restroom to which lockers had been added.

But Mrs. Yelincic wasn't satisfied. "And these men, they don't mind taking orders from a woman?"

Sergeant Campos immediately sprang to mind. "I'm sure some of them do," Marian said. "But we have regulations now—most police departments do anymore. Sexist and racist talk and behavior simply are not tolerated."

Claire pitched in. "Things have changed, Mama."

"And you're telling me all these men obey these regulations?" Mrs. Yelincic made a sound of disbelief. "I know men, and they like to have their own way."

Mr. Yelincic smiled and nodded.

Ivan tried to help. "Hey, I'm a man and I worked with Mar—Lieutenant Larch for years. No problem."

"But she was not your superior then," Razor Blades grated.

Marian patted her mouth with a napkin. "Mrs. Yelincic, if anyone gives me a hard time, I have the authority to take disciplinary action. I can send the offender for counseling, or I can suspend him up to three days without pay. If the unacceptable behavior persists, I can file charges against him and request a hearing. Our regulations have teeth— they're not just a set of guidelines. Do you know how many times I've had to take disciplinary action since I was promoted to lieutenant?" Almost a month now.

"How many?"

"Not once. Not one single time." Marian turned to the nodding, smiling man on her right. "That's a pretty good record, don't you think, Mr. Yelincic?"

Surprised, he stammered, "Oh, uh, yes, yes!"

Satisfied that the man could speak, she turned back to Mrs. Yelincic. "So you see, while it's still a problem, it's now a controllable problem. As Claire said, things have changed."

But Mrs. Yelincic had saved her zinger for last. "Lieutenant

Larch, I want you to tell me the truth now. Will you tell me the truth? Don't lie to me."

Thank you for assuming I'm a liar. "Of course I'll tell you the truth. What's the question?"

Here it came. Her interrogator looked her straight in the eye and said, "Do you really think it's right for women to give orders to men?"

Pin-drop time. Marian laughed easily and winked, and leaned in close to Mrs. Yelincic, woman to woman. "Why not?" she said in a confidential tone. "We've been doing it for centuries."

"Hey, I heard that!" Ivan protested. Claire laughed; Mr. Yelincic did his thing.

And it was all right: Mrs. Yelincic was laughing too. It wasn't true, of course. But to a woman whose life had been lived in service to her family, there was a great deal of satisfaction in hearing outside confirmation that she had really been calling the shots all along. Marian had looked at the ghostly presence of Mr. Yelincic and figured Claire's mother had carved as much authority for herself as it was possible to carve out of the institution called marriage.

It wouldn't be like that for Ivan and Claire, Marian mused. Claire had a life and work she had no intention of abandoning simply because she was married (she was a medical librarian). And Ivan was no easily dominated smiler and nodder. The newlyweds would have problems—but they'd be their own problems, not Claire's parents'.

The table was cleared of dishes and they got down to business. Mrs. Yelincic knew exactly what needed to be done and wasn't shy about saying so. "You know the best man is responsible for seeing everyone gets paid?" she started out. "Except the florist—we pay the florist ahead of time. The caterers, the orchestra . . . oh, I should warn you.

When you give the envelope to Father Kuzak, he's going to hint it isn't enough, as sure as you breathe. But don't you give him one cent more! Do you hear me? Ivan, sit down—this concerns you. How much are you going to give Father Kuzak?"

It went on for over an hour, Marian filling page after page of her notebook. She learned which ushers were prompt and which were not, how many members of the wedding party would need transportation from the church to the reception hall, whose car tended to break down at crucial moments and whose was never quite clean, the exact route that the best man (in the lead car) was to take, precisely the right moment to toast the bride and groom, and on and on. This was one wedding in which nothing would be left to chance, and Marian was heartily glad of it.

When finally she got up to leave, Marian felt confident about the upcoming wedding for the first time now that she knew what needed to be done—and it was all Mrs. Yelincic's doing. She told her so.

The older woman couldn't have been more pleased. "Why, you're welcome, Lieutenant, I'm sure. I'm glad to help."

Marian laughed easily. "You did more than help, Mrs. Yelincic—you saved my neck."

"Please—call me Aphra."

"Gladly, Aphra. And my name is Marian."

"Well, Marian, you must come back to see us again before the wedding."

"I'll certainly do that. And thank you again."

Mr. Yelincic smiled and nodded.

Claire was going back into Manhattan with them, so Marian climbed into the backseat of Ivan's car. As they pulled away, Ivan said, "That was good, telling her to call you Marian. Now she can brag to all her friends that she's on a first-name basis with a lieutenant of the police."

Claire added, "And you'd be amazed at the number of times she's going to work your name into a conversation."

"Ivan," Marian said, "would you have asked me to be your best man if I were still a sergeant?"

He took so much time thinking it over that Claire laughed and slapped at his shoulder. "Well," he conceded, "we might have let you be flower girl."

Marian sighed. "Shut up and drive," she said.

* 17 *

Marian awoke the next morning to the sound of flutes playing Bach.

She opened one eye and stared suspiciously at the unfamiliar clock radio; where was the customary brassy alarm that got her up and going every morning? Her waking disorientation passed; she rolled over to see that Holland was awake and in the process of sitting up. "I spent the night?"

He nodded gravely. "You spent the night."

"Hm. Didn't mean to do that."

"I know. You came for a quick roll in the hay and goodbye."

"Is that what I came for?"

"Isn't it?"

"Holland, don't ask me to figure things out before coffee."

He fingered a strand of her hair. "Why don't you ever call me by my first name?"

She rolled over and threw a leg over him. "Too personal."

He laughed. "Well, don't expect me to call you 'Larch'—that's what Saint Murtaugh calls you, isn't it?"

She moaned. "Murtaugh. What time is it?"

"Six-thirty, a little after."

"I've got to get home, shower, change. Grumble grumble."

He cleared his throat. "And you're going to have a new

problem to contend with before you leave unless you move that leg—and I mean right now."

Marian moved her leg. "Where are my shoes?" She found one under the bed and the other out in the hall. She dressed hurriedly; Holland got up to help and of course just slowed her down. She told him to stand with his hands behind his back until she was gone. With a sardonic smile, he obeyed.

All the way home, into the shower, into fresh clothes—Marian was puzzled. She'd accepted the fact that Holland was going to play a part in her life and was surprised to find how lacking in trauma such acceptance had proved to be. She'd been happy last night, in the big bed with him. She'd felt at peace.

But.

She'd put it out of her mind last night, but now she couldn't help but think about it. His apartment. The first time she'd seen it, it had been spartanly furnished; only the barest necessities were there. It was the temporary resting place of a sojourner, someone used to moving quickly and often. But now it was the place of a man who planned on staying a while. Holland had spared no expense to make his nest comfortable and . . . well, beautiful. He'd surrounded himself with luxury—the ostentatious kind, the sort that called attention to itself. The apartment itself was on Central Park West, not exactly a low-rent district.

And his agency offices shrieked money. The costly equipment, the operating expenses . . . his monthly payroll alone must be a backbreaker. André Flood and at least two other "computer detectives" she'd seen there. The receptionist, Mrs. Grainger. Was Zoe Esterhaus his only street operative? Marian doubted it.

Where did the money come from?

He couldn't have saved enough from his few years as an FBI agent. It was possible he'd taken out loans for start-up money, but what had he used for collateral? He owned nothing that Marian knew of. Had a venture capitalist provided seed money?

Or had Holland sat down at his computer, touched the right keys, and simply transferred the funds he needed from elsewhere to his own accounts?

That was the problem: Marian could easily believe he had done just that. He had the knowhow, and he showed precious little compunction about sticking his electronic nose into places it didn't belong. Holland had always been a bit shady; and as much as Marian wanted to believe he was legit, she never could, quite.

Always between them was this question of trust. Marian simply couldn't bring herself to trust him, and that was that. Ironically, it was the question of trust that had attracted him to her in the first place. Marian was no beauty; she didn't kid herself that Holland lay awake at night fantasizing about her. It was only when he began to suspect that he had at last found someone he could trust that Holland had been drawn to her.

What had happened to him that had caused the need for trust to dominate his life so? Whatever it was—and Marian speculated it was a continuing series of things rather than one big dramatic act of treachery—it had made him oversensitive on the subject . . . downright touchy, in fact. He'd seen her choosing to stay with the police instead of working with him as an act of betrayal; she was only now beginning to understand how much she'd hurt him in making that choice. But he seemed to have overcome that distrustful interpretation of her choosing; his sending her the keys to his apartment, to his private space—that was probably the biggest gesture of trust he'd made since he was a child. The significance of the gesture was not lost on Marian.

Time to get to the bottom of this. In the stationhouse, Marian stopped by Dowd's desk long enough to write on a notepad lying there. "Something I want you to check out."

Dowd tore off the top sheet and read the name. "Curt Holland?"

"A private investigator. He has his own agency—Zoe Esterhaus works for him."

"Oh yeah. The Knowles case."

"I want you to find out what his prior experience was that qualified him to take the state licensing exam. If he apprenticed with a licensed investigator, I want to know who."

"Priority?"

"Low."

Dowd nodded and placed the sheet of paper on top of a pile of others awaiting his attention. "Er, Campos wants to see you. When you have time." He looked uneasy.

"I have time now. Where is he?"

"Men's room. I'll get him."

She'd barely had time to get her coat off and settle before Sergeant Campos came in. His face was tight. "Looks like you were right," he said neutrally.

Marian did a quick mental run through the cases he was handling and picked the right one. "Sanderson is a fence?"

"Walker and Dowd followed him to a warehouse on South Street," the sergeant said. "They were unloading big appliances—televisions, computers, even refrigerators, fer gawd's sake. That shop of his just handles little stuff, nothing bigger than a tape recorder."

"Why South Street? Shipping overseas? Importing?"

"We don't know yet. But I think we got enough for a search warrant."

Marian nodded. "See Captain Murtaugh. Tell him I said it was a go. Good work, Campos."

He grunted acknowledgement and left. No sooner was he gone than Dowd came in. "Lieutenant?"

"Yes?"

"About Sanderson—me and Walker, we just read him wrong. We thought if he was into fencing, it was just small stuff and only once in a while . . . junk, like, a kinda sideline. We can't spend time on every little bit of petty larceny we learn about, Lieutenant. That's why we let it slide. We were wrong and the guy is into big-time fencing, but we didn't know that."

"Relax, Dowd," Marian said, "I'm not charging you with dereliction of duty. I know you have to let the small stuff slide. God knows I've done it myself often enough. But either you or Walker should have noticed the guy's clothes."

He cocked his head at her. "That's really all you had to go on? His clothes?"

"That and his expensive manicure and the gold watch he was wearing. He's bound to dress down for his shop. But when you brought him in for questioning, you'd picked him up at a restaurant, hadn't you? You and Walker both know to pay attention to the way people adorn themselves. You got a little lax."

Dowd sighed. "Yeah, I guess we did. Sorry, Lieutenant. It won't happen again."

Marian nodded and waved him out.

Quickly she read through the reports that appeared magically on her desk every time she was out of the office. She went to an interrogation room and listened as two of Sergeant Buchanan's detectives put a suspected dealer through the paces. Then she rounded up Perlmutter and O'Toole.

Old business first. "Perlmutter, did you find out why Oliver Knowles and his wife had separated?"

"I don't think the son knows," he answered. "Austin Knowles said they just drifted apart."

"Well, it's probably not pertinent anyway." On to new business. "A full background check on David Unger," she said. "Finances, personal life, ties with the Knowles family. What he did before working at O.K. Toys."

"Then he *is* our suspect?"

"You got a better prospect?"

"Nope."

"Then we're going to look into Mr. Unger's life until we find something that tells us we're wasting our time." She caught the expression on Perlmutter's face. "Something wrong?"

He said, "Lieutenant, I'd like to run a background check on Elmore Zook too. He's just too much in the thick of things. He represented Oliver Knowles and now he's representing Knowles's son as well as Unger in the sale of shares they're working on—I know it's all family stuff, but it doesn't smell right."

"What smells wrong?"

"Zook himself," Perlmutter said. "The man's just too . . . calm. Too sure of himself. If he was arrogant or liked to play one-upmanship games, well, that's what you expect in high-powered types. But this guy gives the impression that he knows things the rest of the world isn't allowed to know. Sort of like he's saying that he's safe no matter what."

O'Toole said, "That's a good description of Unger too."

"And probably of Oliver Knowles as well," Marian murmured. "All right, Perlmutter, go ahead with it."

"Where'll you be, Lieutenant?"

"If we're going to make David Unger our prime suspect," she said, "then I think it's time I met the gentleman. I'll be at O.K. Toys."

* 18 *

O'Toole was right: not a toy visible anywhere at O.K. Toys.

Marian mentioned this casually to David Unger's secretary when asking to see the boss. The secretary, a smartly turned-out woman in her late forties, had sighed with regret and said the place used to be filled with toys. But once Mr. Knowles stopped manufacturing his own and switched to distribution only, there really wasn't much point in displaying the vendors' toys. New models came out every month now, for one thing. The market had changed drastically the past few years; no one any longer even tried to make toys that could be passed down to the next generation. It seemed to Marian that the woman's regret was sincere.

The suite of offices in the Flatiron Building was smaller than Marian had expected and looked like any ordinary business office on a budget. "A lot of people had to be laid off, I suppose," she said. "When Mr. Knowles stopped manufacturing, I mean."

"There weren't all that many workers left," the secretary said. "The factory in New Jersey was the only one still operating, and it was a small one. Mr. Knowles had been cutting back gradually for several years before he decided to make the switch."

"Why did he switch?"

She smiled, a little sadly. "Age, mostly. And even though he never said so to me, I think he was disillusioned with the market for toys. All those breakable plastics, you know."

Marian didn't but nodded as if she did. "When was the last time you saw Mr. Knowles?"

"Oh . . . three or four days before he died, I think. He still came in about once a week."

It all sounded so up-and-up that Marian was beginning to suspect O'Toole had been reading something fishy into O.K. Toys that simply wasn't there; perennial pitfall for the rookie detective. David Unger was in a meeting, his secretary said; she notified him Lieutenant Larch of the NYPD was there.

Marian waited only a few minutes before a door opened and a fortyish man with a luxurious mustache and longish brown hair stepped into the reception area. He was poised, well-dressed, pleasantly professional in his manner. "Lieutenant Larch? I'm David Unger."

"Mr. Unger. I'd like to talk to you about Oliver Knowles."

"I spoke to a Detective O'Toole yesterday. I told him everything I know."

Marian doubted that. "Just a few minutes of your time, please."

"Of course." He gestured toward the door he'd just come through. "We can talk in here."

Marian thought the door would lead to his private office, but instead it opened into a small conference room. Two people were seated at the circular table, Austin Knowles and a man Marian had never seen before. Knowles rose when she came in and asked, "Do you have any news for me, Lieutenant?"

"Not yet, Mr. Knowles."

Before Oliver Knowles's son could say anything else, David

Unger stepped in smoothly and said, "Lieutenant, this is Elmore Zook. Mr. Zook handles the company's legal affairs."

The lawyer was also on his feet, a bald, stout man in his sixties with the same easy manner that David Unger had; Austin Knowles was the only tense one in the room. "Lieutenant," Zook was saying, "if there's anything we can do to help, just say the word."

"Well, what do you know about professional hit men?" Marian asked, taking the chair Unger offered her.

Zook smiled wryly as all three men resumed their seats. "Very little, I'm afraid. You're convinced it was a hired killing?"

"No question of that. The question is *why*."

"It had to be a mistake," Unger interposed. "There's no reason anyone would want Oliver dead. The killer shot the wrong man."

Zook nodded. "That's the only explanation."

Well, no, it's not. "Who's Rosalind Bowman?" she threw at them.

"Who?" Austin Knowles said. The other two looked the same question at her.

"Rosalind Bowman. She's a woman who has disappeared— voluntarily. She's undoubtedly left the city by now. But before she left, she hired a detective agency to follow Oliver Knowles and report on his activities."

"What?" Austin Knowles was on his feet again. "Why did she do that?"

"I was hoping you could tell me," Marian replied.

"How the hell can I tell you when I never heard of the woman?"

"Austin," Zook said mildly. The architect sat back down. "That's interesting, Lieutenant. What was the connection between Oliver and this Bowman woman?"

"That's what I'm trying to find out." Holland had said

Rosalind Bowman formerly worked in radio and television, but there must be some connection to Knowles. Marian turned to Unger. "Did she ever work here?"

"Not that I know of." Unger pressed a button on the intercom on the table. "Iris, I need you to check our personnel records. See if we ever had a Rosalind Bowman on the payroll . . . Bowman, that's right." He turned back to Marian and waited—pleasantly cooperative, offering nothing.

Marian tried another tack. "What am I interrupting here? The transfer of stock?"

"You're not interrupting," Unger said easily. "We've finished everything except the signing of the agreements."

"Do you have any objection to telling me how the stock is distributed now?"

Unger didn't quite smile as he said, "Elmore, do we have any objection to telling her?"

Zook did smile though. "No, we don't have any objection to telling her." He turned to Marian. "Before Oliver died, Austin, Dave, and I each owned ten percent. Oliver held the rest. Austin inherits his dad's shares, but he doesn't want to run the company. So he's selling a few shares to me and most of the rest to Dave. Now Austin and I each hold fifteen percent, and Dave will have the other seventy. It's Dave's company now." The lawyer was well satisfied. "We've agreed on a payment schedule."

"Congratulations, Mr. Unger," Marian said tonelessly. "I understand you've pretty much been running the company the last few years."

"Pretty much," Unger agreed. "Oliver was still contributing, though. He never stopped having ideas. But he no longer dealt with the day-to-day details of the business."

"What about Oliver Knowles's wife? Did she never own a percentage?"

A momentary silence, and then Austin Knowles said, "No. She and my father were estranged. Dad had been supporting her all these years, but she didn't own shares in the company."

"Why were your parents separated, Mr. Knowles?"

"Really, Lieutenant," Zook protested. "That's a highly personal matter."

"Yes, it is," she agreed. "Why, Mr. Knowles?"

He spread his hands. "Why do any two people separate? People change. They didn't even like each other anymore. There was no reason for them to stay together."

"Who changed the most? Your mother or your father?"

"That's a little hard for me to say," Knowles answered tightly, "since I didn't know them before I was born."

Zook spoke up again. "Austin has been through a terrible experience, Lieutenant Larch. Raking up old troubles is painful for him—can't you see? And how could his parents' past marital problems have anything to do with what happened on that bus? Far be it from me to tell you how to do your job, but it seems to me you should be looking for the man who pulled the trigger."

"Yes, once you find him," Unger said, "you can work a deal with him. Reduced sentence in exchange for the name of the man who hired him. Isn't that how you work these things?"

Zook nodded. "It's standard procedure. Your shooter will give up the name to shorten his time—there's no honor among thieves, folk wisdom to the contrary." The other two nodded with him.

They're humoring me, Marian thought, both amazed and annoyed. "The one thing I do see," she said, "is that the only three people who profited from Oliver Knowles's death are sitting right here in this room."

A stunned silence while three formerly pleasant faces lost their pleasantness. "Are you out of your mind?" Austin Knowles asked softly.

"I don't think so. You inherited a lot of loot, Mr. Knowles. You'll make money on the sale of your shares to Mr. Unger. I've seen your father's apartment—the contents are worth a small fortune, not to mention the value of the apartment itself. There could be even more, for all I know. Investments, perhaps."

"That's ridiculous!"

She turned to David Unger. "And you, Mr. Unger . . . you now own the company where only last week you were just a salaried employee. People have killed for a lot less than that." Finally she looked at the third man. "Even you, Mr. Zook. Your holdings just jumped fifty percent. Fifteen percent now instead of ten."

If he was angry, he was careful not to let it show. "Do you think I'd kill a friend of nearly forty years for a lousy five percent of his company?"

"I don't know, Mr. Zook. Would you?"

"This is absurd!" Unger protested with a half laugh. "I would have ended up with control of the company eventually anyway. I didn't need to kill to get it."

"And you really think I could have killed my own father?" Austin Knowles asked. "A man dies, someone inherits, the police suspect the heir. One, two, three. Just like that."

"All right, then," Marian said, unfazed, "tell me who else benefited. The only one I've learned of who had no use for Oliver Knowles was his wife, and she'd been dead for a month when he was shot—she didn't order the hit. Maybe Lucas Novak suddenly got tired of his cushy life. Maybe he didn't want to be Oliver Knowles's personal secretary any longer and put an end to it by having his benefactor killed.

Or maybe you think the housekeeper suddenly went berserk and put an ad in the paper saying 'Killer Wanted'—do you think that's what happened? *That's* what's absurd. Who else could it be? If you know somebody, give me a name!"

Zook protested, "Oliver had hundreds of business contacts. Any one of them could have done it."

"He was retired. No longer a player. Why kill him now?"

Just then the door opened and Unger's secretary stepped into the room. "Mr. Unger, no one named Rosalind Bowman ever worked for O.K. Toys."

"Thank you, Iris," he said automatically. She withdrew. Unger was playing with his mustache, the first nervous mannerism he'd shown.

"What about her, the Bowman woman?" Austin Knowles asked. "She could have done it."

"Then why did she hire a private detective to follow your father at the same time she hired a gunman to kill him?"

A pause. "To check up on the gunman? To make sure he did the job?"

Marian shook her head. "Rosalind Bowman has disappeared, remember. The detective wasn't able to report back to her."

"So she learned about the shooting from the newspaper. She didn't need to ask the detective."

"You're grasping at straws, Mr. Knowles."

An uncomfortable silence grew in the room. David Unger stood up and went over to gaze out the window. "You truly believe one of us had Oliver killed?"

Marian said nothing, waiting.

Unger turned back from the window. "Then I'm probably at the top of your list of suspects. You think I wanted O.K. Toys so much I killed the company's founder to get it. That's what you think, isn't it?"

"The thought has occurred to me."

"Lieutenant, the killer shot the *wrong man*." Implied: *Can't you get that through your thick head?* "Are hit men infallible? Don't they ever make mistakes?"

"Mr. Unger, there was no one else on that bus who matched Oliver Knowles's description." No need to mention the passengers who escaped before the police got there. "The killer made no mistake. Oliver Knowles was his target."

That sounded like a good exit line, so Marian stood up to leave. She'd wanted to shake these three big shots up a bit but wasn't able to gauge how successful she'd been. Austin Knowles appeared agitated; but then, he'd been agitated the other time she'd talked to him. Zook and Unger just stared at her blankly.

"I'll be talking to you again," she said pleasantly, and left.

19

Marian used her car phone to call Kelly Ingram. "Lunchtime, toots. Are you up to facing food? I can pick something up."

"Soup," Kelly's voice said thickly. "Bring soup."

"Soup it is," Marian said cheerfully, and disconnected. Kelly didn't really start to perk until about midafternoon. Her friend always needed to unwind after an evening performance and rarely got to bed before the wee hours. Marian stopped at a deli and got two different kinds of soup; a choice was always nice.

No parking place in Kelly's block, so Marian had to walk back a ways. She was approaching the building where Kelly lived, doing her usual cop thing of checking out the neighborhood, when a figure standing in a doorway across the street caught her eye. A familiar figure at that.

Marian darted through the traffic and hurried to where the figure was standing. "Hello, Carla."

Carla Banner did a double take—and then remembered Marian. "Oh, you're Kelly's friend," she said effusively. "I remember you. At Gallagher's, right? But I don't know your name." She actually simpered. "Kelly forgot to introduce us."

"The name is Larch," Marian said, taking out her badge

and showing it to the young woman. "Lieutenant Larch, NYPD. That's *police*, Carla."

She took a step back. "I didn't do anything wrong."

"You're doing something wrong right now," Marian said. "Kelly told you to stop following her."

"I'm not bothering her! She doesn't even know I'm out here."

"She will as soon as I tell her. Is Kelly going to have to get a restraining order? Will she have to go to court to make you stop?"

Carla gaped. "Can she really do that? Get a restraining order?"

Probably not. "Of course she can. Is that what you want? You're making her hate you, you know."

Carla looked shocked. "I don't want her to hate me! I want, I want . . ."

"You want her to like you. To make you part of her life. But you can't force yourself on people, Carla. You wait for an invitation. And Kelly has made it quite clear she doesn't want you hanging around. So, take off, Carla. And don't come back."

If looks could kill, Marian would have dropped dead on the spot. Carla muttered something under her breath, but turned away and slouched off down the street.

Marian waited until she was out of sight and then crossed to Kelly's building. Once Kelly had buzzed her in, she told her friend about Carla's lurking across the street.

"Aw, gawd," Kelly said, taking the soup cartons out of their paper bag. "She does know where I live after all. Shit." She opened the cartons. "Lima bean or beef veggie?"

"I don't care."

Kelly took the lima bean, pouring both soups into bowls. "I don't know what to do about her, Marian."

"I chased her off for now, but she'll be back. And there's nothing the police can do, because she hasn't broken any laws. Maybe you should take Ian Cavanaugh's advice. Try yelling and screaming."

Kelly swallowed her soup. "Even tepid, that tastes good." She ate some more. "Maybe that's what I should do. Every time I see her from now on, I should just tell her loudly to go away and leave me alone. Maybe I can *embarrass* her into stopping."

"Worth a try."

"I called you after the performance last night, but you weren't home."

"I was at Holland's."

Kelly digested that, nodded. "So he's back, then."

"Looks like it."

"Well . . . good luck. At least you'll never get bored."

Just then Marian's beeper sounded. She used Kelly's phone to call in. She finished quickly and reached for her coat. "Captain wants me. Toot sweet."

Kelly poured the rest of Marian's soup back into its carton. "Can you eat cold soup and drive at the same time?"

"I'm an expert at it."

No sign of Carla Banner down on the street. Marian finished her soup just as she arrived at the Midtown South precinct building.

Upstairs, Captain Murtaugh was waiting for her. "You've rattled a cage," he said by way of greeting.

That was fast. "I sincerely hope so. Who complained?"

"Elmore Zook. I've been ordered to tell you you'd better be damned sure of your facts before you start accusing prominent men like Elmore Zook of murder. Are you sure?"

"Nope." She held up a finger. "But I didn't accuse him. I merely pointed out that he was one of the only three people who benefited from Oliver Knowles's death."

"Uh-huh!" Murtaugh was satisfied with this observance of the letter of the law, if not its intent. "Who are the other two?"

"Austin Knowles and David Unger."

"Austin Knowles . . . the dead man's son? He's a suspect?"

Marian sighed. "Yeah, I'm having trouble with that one. I'd say Dave Unger is our most likely suspect."

"That reminds me. The DA's office says they can have an accountant at O.K. Toys this afternoon."

"That soon!" Marian was pleased. "I suppose it's too much to hope that Unger's been skimming off the top. But that whole place seems to be just a going-through-the-motions operation. Something not quite right there."

"Any theories?"

Marian shrugged. "O'Toole suggested a money-laundering front. But that's just a guess."

"Might be a good one. Keep me posted."

She left, running over in her mind what needed to be done that afternoon. She walked right past Dowd's desk without seeing the paper he was holding out to her.

"Lieutenant! That PI you wanted me to check out?"

"What?" She focused on him with an effort.

"Curt Holland. He did apprentice with a licensed detective, name of Constantine Philippides." He handed her the paper. "Now deceased. Died seven years ago."

She took the paper with her into the office, staring at it while hanging her coat on the rack. Constantine Philippides. Who the hell was he? Dead seven years: not the source of information about Holland she'd hoped for. Who'd been around a long time and might know about Constantine Philippides?

Marian stepped out of her office and looked around; no Sergeant Buchanan. She left a note on his desk to see her.

She went back to her desk and tried to think of another way of going at the Oliver Knowles case. Knowles had gone to Lionel Madison Trains the day he was killed; the staff there all knew Knowles. *One of our best customers*, they'd said. He'd left his gloves there, that last day. Did Knowles pay by credit card? By check? Oh no, they said. They were always paid in cash on delivery. Was that the usual way they did business? No, but they all knew Mr. Knowles. Who actually paid them? Mr. Knowles's secretary, Lucas Novak.

Marian had Perlmutter and O'Toole over at Knowles's apartment at that very moment, going through the dead man's private papers. They'd had to get a warrant, since Lucas Novak and Ellen Rudolph—Mrs. R—were still living there; the secretary had already called once to complain. Marian specifically wanted to know how much cash business Knowles had done—and whether it looked as if he had been trying to avoid leaving a paper trail.

Or whether she was chasing shadows.

An hour later, Sergeant Buchanan stuck his head through the doorway. "You want to see me?"

"Come in, Buchanan. Question for you. Did you ever run across a private investigator named Constantine Philippides?"

Buchanan laughed shortly. "Connie the Greek." He sat down heavily. "Yeah, I knew Connie. Died five, six years ago. Why?"

"What can you tell me about him? What kind of investigator was he?"

"Low-rent. He started out okay, but . . . Connie was a lush, Lieutenant. Drank himself into the gutter. You know how he died? Pothole got him. Not even a very big pothole. But we'd just had a good rain and it was full of water—thass all it took. Connie was sailin' three sheets to the wind and tripped over his own feet and went in face-first. Nobody stopped to help. Nobody thought that a guy layin' in an alley with his face in a puddle might be in trouble. Connie the Greek drowned in three inches of rainwater."

"God." Hell of a way to go; poor Connie, whatever his failings. "Was he bent?"

"Musta been. He was pretty hard up for cash, last time I saw him. Gettin' desperate."

"But did he take bribes?"

"What did Connie have that anyone—oh, you mean like for givin' perjured testimony? Wouldn't surprise me."

"What if someone wanted to skip the apprenticeship period required for private investigators and go straight to the state exam? He'd need written evidence of prior experience he didn't have. Would Connie have signed the necessary papers? For a fee?"

Buchanan raised his shaggy eyebrows. "Nice scam. Yeah, Connie woulda gone along. Don't take much effort to sign a few papers. You know somebody did that, Lieutenant?"

"Just a suspicion. No proof."

At that moment a bass voice boomed out from the squadroom, "Buchanan! Line two."

Buchanan pointed at Marian's phone. "D'ya mind, Lieutenant?"

"Go ahead."

The sergeant's baggy face tensed as he took his phone call. He pulled Marian's notepad toward him and started jotting down details. "Yeah . . . yeah. Got it. Thanks for lettin' me know." He hung up and looked at Marian. "Do you remember Robin Muller?"

The name rang a bell. "Remind me."

"NYU grad student. Boyfriend reported her missin'."

Marian remembered. "They live in the Ninth Precinct."

"That's the one. Well, she's turned up. Dead."

Something in the way he was saying it made her sit up. "And?"

"She was killed on the subway. Train full of people. Someone put a silenced gun up against her and pulled the trigger." And in case Marian didn't get it, he added, "Just like Oliver Knowles."

* 20 *

Robin Muller had been riding the IRT when she was shot shortly before the train pulled into Astor Place Station. The subway car was crowded, but Robin Muller had had a seat. Only when the train swerved around a curve had she pitched forward against the standing passengers, the open copy of *Sports Illustrated* propped on her lap falling away to reveal the spreading bloodstain on her torso.

But this time—*this* time—the killer had not been so lucky. Several people had noticed the hook-nosed man who'd elbowed aside a woman carrying dry cleaning to grab the seat next to Muller when it became available . . . only to get up again almost immediately.

"This could be the breakthrough we need," Captain Murtaugh said as uniformed officers kept gawkers away from the halted subway car where Robin Muller's body lay.

"Mighty costly breakthrough," Marian murmured, looking down at the dead girl. Robin Muller had been pretty, with short black hair curling loosely around her face. She was young . . . so very young! An unlived life. Muller had bled heavily, the blood seeping all the way through the army jacket she was wearing and already turned black.

Sergeant Buchanan knelt by the body and pushed up

Muller's sleeves. "No track marks. The boyfriend said she was a health nut."

Murtaugh asked, "Buck, how did you get in on this?"

"I was the one the boyfriend talked to when he reported her missin'," Buchanan explained.

The captain nodded. "Larch, I want a cap put on this one. If the killer learns we've got a description, he's going to be long gone."

"Right." She stepped off the car to the platform to give the instructions. The train was stopped in Astor Place Station. Several of the officers were herding witnesses toward the stairs, to take them in for a session with a graphic arts technician. One of them was complaining loudly that he'd miss his appointment. The Crime Scene Unit came bustling in, kvetching about a delivery-truck breakdown that had backed up traffic for blocks.

Marian followed the CSU back into the subway car to find Buchanan telling Murtaugh that the boyfriend had said Muller had been pretty flush these past few months, but he didn't know where the money came from. "Captain, we gotta find that boyfriend."

"We got the boyfriend," a familiar voice said.

They all turned to look at the dark-skinned woman who had come up behind them unnoticed.

"Gloria?" Marian said, pleasantly surprised. "This is your case?"

"Mine and Roberts's." Gloria Sanchez jerked a thumb toward her partner, who could be seen through the subway car window talking to a distraught-looking young man. "Hello, Captain Murtaugh."

"Good to see you again, Detective."

Marian introduced the Ninth Precinct detective to Buchanan, who asked, "Howja find the boyfriend so quick?"

"He was waitin' for her here."

The boyfriend's name was Larry Hibler. He'd told Gloria Sanchez that Robin Muller had been staying with a friend in Brooklyn, afraid to call him because she thought the phone might be tapped. She'd finally gotten word to him through a mutual friend: be at a certain pay phone at a certain hour and she'd call.

The call had come at the designated time. Hibler said Muller had been scared to death. She'd told him she was in deep shit, that someone was after her; she'd mentioned the name Virgil. Mentioned how? She'd said Virgil would send someone, Hibler replied. The paymaster had warned her—spitefully, she said. What paymaster? Where did she work? Larry Hibler had hemmed and hawed and admitted he didn't know she'd been working at all.

Marian stared. "They were living together and he didn't know she was working?"

Gloria Sanchez shrugged. "That's what he says."

At any rate, Hibler had convinced Muller that she couldn't hide out for the rest of her life. Afraid to go to the police and afraid not to, she'd agreed to meet him and talk it over, to try to decide what to do. They were to meet at Astor Place; she didn't dare return home.

"A description of the shooter and a name for the man who sent him," Captain Murtaugh said with satisfaction. "As well as a third man—this paymaster, whoever he is. Now we've got something to go on."

The Crime Scene Unit told them more or less politely they were in the way and they moved outside to the station platform. "Captain," Marian said, "I know two shootings don't make a pattern—oh hell, yes, they do! We need—"

"A computer search for the MO," he finished for her. "I'll put in a request. Sanchez, is Captain DiFalco in his office?"

"He was when I left."

"I'm going to make this a joint investigation. Larch, I want a report when you're finished here." He turned and headed up the stairs to the street.

A number of Transit Authority officials were there, trying to hurry the police so they could get the train running again before rush hour hit. Marian spared a thought for all the shuttling and diverting that was going on to keep the regularly scheduled trains from plowing into the uncharacteristically stationary one. A blue-suit came down to say the crowd on the street was getting ugly and they could use some help keeping them out of the subway station. Gloria Sanchez sent her partner to call for back-up.

Buchanan said to Sanchez, "I know the lieutenant here used to work outa the Ninth—but how'd you know Captain Murtaugh?"

"Worked a case for him once," she replied laconically.

"Midtown South borrowed her," Marian added. "Gloria, Sergeant Buchanan is going to act as liaison on this case. And I'll send you copies of our reports on the Knowles shooting. But right now I'd like a word with Larry Hibler."

"If he's still able to talk."

Hibler was slumped down on the concrete floor, his back against a pillar. About Robin Muller's age, thin, pale. His face was a mixture of confusion and pain.

Marian hunkered down beside him. "Hello, Larry. My name is Lieutenant Larch. I'm sorry to bother you at a time like this, but there are a couple of things I have to ask you."

He gave her an unfocused look. "Larch. That's a tree."

"Yes, it is." She paused, and then asked, "Did Robin ever mention the name Oliver Knowles to you?"

Hibler frowned in concentration, shook his head.

"What about Rosalind Bowman?"

"No."

"Who's that?" Gloria demanded.

"Bowman hired Holland's agency to follow Knowles. But now she's disappeared."

"Oh yeah," Gloria said. "I heard there was a private op on that bus."

Marian turned back to Larry Hibler. "Are you sure you don't know those names? Oliver Knowles. Rosalind Bowman. Think back."

He shook his head again. "I never heard of them. Oh, man, I didn't even know she was working."

The remark struck Marian as out of context. "What about this Virgil? Did Robin ever tell you about him?"

"I never even heard the name before today. On the phone. The last time I talked to her." He started crying.

Marian put a comforting hand on his shoulder. After a minute she withdrew it and stood up. She said to Gloria, "Have you called for a graphics tech?"

"Right before you got here. He should be at the station-house by now. Wanna come? Gotta get those descriptions while they're fresh."

"Yes, we're coming."

At that moment two men from the Medical Examiner's office rolled a wheeled stretcher off the subway car, its body bag strapped into place. Larry Hibler, sitting with his head drooping on his chest, didn't see. One of the Transit Authority officials came hurrying up to Gloria Sanchez. She held up a hand to forestall him. "Let 'em get the body out first," she said softly. "Then you can open for business." The man grunted and turned away.

Marian and Buchanan watched as Gloria gentled Larry Hibler to his feet, explaining that they'd need a statement from him but that could wait until tomorrow. She signaled a bluesuit to drive him home.

The three detectives followed them up the stairs to the street. The crowd of frustrated passengers had fallen momentarily silent when the corpse in its body bag was trundled past. Gloria told the officers guarding the entrance to the subway to let them in.

"Where's Roberts?" Gloria asked, looking around for her partner as the crowd surged past them down the subway steps. "Hey, Marian, if you're lucky Captain DiFalco will still be there. You can catch up on old times."

Marian rolled her eyes.

Buchanan watched the exchange with interest. "Don't get along with your old captain?" he asked Marian with a grin.

"It's nothing serious," she said. "We merely hate each other's guts, that's all."

"I'd laugh," Gloria said heavily, "but I'm still stuck with him."

"And whose fault is that?" Marian asked unsympathetically. "As long as you refuse to take the Sergeants Exam, you're going to stay right where you are."

"Don't start."

"I've already started. We're short a sergeant at Midtown South right now. I'd put in a personal request for you myself. And Captain Murtaugh would add his own request, I'm sure."

"Hey, I told you before. I don't wanna be no sergeant."

"What's wrong with being a sergeant?" Sergeant Buchanan asked.

"I don't wanna talk about it, okay?" Gloria was adamant.

Her partner chose that moment to come running up, out of breath. "Back-up is on the . . . way." His voice faded as he saw people going into the subway entrance.

"Great timing, Roberts," Gloria said sardonically. "You

better stay here and tell 'em they're not needed. We're going to the stationhouse."

"Shit," Roberts said.

Gloria turned to leave and called back over her shoulder to Marian, "You know the way."

"Unfortunately," Marian said with a sigh. "Come on, Buchanan."

They headed toward their car, leaving Detective Roberts standing by the subway entrance and glowering at a world that moved faster than he did.

* 21 *

Marian drove. The distance between Astor Place and the Ninth Precinct stationhouse was short and she could probably have driven it in her sleep.

Buchanan cleared his throat. "Lieutenant, I know this is outa line—but can you tell me what to expect from this Captain DiFalco? If I'm gonna be the liaison, I gotta know what I'm walkin' into here."

Marian didn't think the question out of line, although Buchanan was clearly uncomfortable asking one superior officer about another. "DiFalco has all the necessary stuff to make a good cop," she said. "He's smart, he's quick, he's observant. He has a way of burrowing through extraneous detail and putting his finger on precisely the one thing that matters."

"So what's the problem?" Buchanan asked.

"The problem is ambition," Marian answered tightly. "He's let it get out of hand. DiFalco's more interested in building up his record of cases solved than he is in making sure the right perp is behind bars."

Buchanan whistled two notes. "One of those, huh."

"It's what we had our final falling-out about," she went on. "It was a big case, an important one. And so compli-cated that Major Crimes wouldn't touch it. Have you ever heard of that happening before? DiFalco wanted to bust that one so bad it was killing him. So he fingered one man, declared the case closed, and called a press conference. And all the time I kept yelling that he had the wrong guy. DiFalco didn't like that."

"Who was right?"

Marian gave him a big grin.

Buchanan laughed. "Which made him love you all the more. Okay, I get the picture."

They pulled into the police parking lot across the street from the Ninth Precinct stationhouse on East Fifth Street. To her bemusement, Marian found she didn't want to go in. There were people still working there that she knew and liked, but the place just had too many bad associations for her.

It was strange. The desk sergeant was surprised to see her, started to say "Hey, Marian," and changed it at the last second to "Hello, Lieutenant." She got that same awkward reaction from everyone she knew. She spoke pleasantly and called everyone by name—the ones she could remember. Buchanan took it all in, said nothing.

Gloria Sanchez was on the phone when they went into the detectives' crowded squadroom. Marian perched on the corner of Gloria's desk and waited until she'd hung up. "Is the graphics tech here?" she asked, looking around.

"We had to put her in the lieutenant's office," Gloria said. "No room out here. Let's go—uh-oh."

Marian turned her head to see Captain DiFalco headed their way.

He stopped about a foot away from Marian. "Lieutenant."

She stood up as gracefully as she could in the space he left her, forcing him to take a step back. "Captain."

"Murtaugh just left," DiFalco said. "We're going to make

this a joint Ninth Precinct/Midtown South investigation. It's official now."

Marian introduced Sergeant Buchanan. "The sergeant will be acting as liaison."

DiFalco barely spared him a glance. "We need your reports on the Knowles shooting and we need them now."

She counted to ten. "I've already told Gloria we'll forward our reports."

"Today, Lieutenant. I want this thing nailed down."

Marian smiled, with her mouth. "Oddly enough, Captain, that's what we want too." Reminding him she was no longer under his command.

"Don't get sarcastic with me, Larch," the captain snapped. "You may have moved uptown, but you're on *my* turf now. I call the shots here."

Feel my muscles? "You and Captain Murtaugh, yes. On this case."

He dismissed Murtaugh with a wave of his hand. "Just get those reports over here!" He charged away.

"Aye, aye, Captain," Marian said to his retreating back.

Gloria waited until DiFalco was out of sight and then hugged herself in an exaggerated shiver. "Brrr. Somebody turn up the heat."

"Yeah," Buchanan agreed, "the temperature did drop about twenty degrees, dinnit?"

"What are you, a comedy team?" Marian growled. "Let's go see what the tech's got."

The lieutenant's office where the graphics tech was working was smaller even than Marian's office. The three witnesses who'd said they could describe the man who'd sat next to Robin Muller on the subway were crowded around the woman seated before her laptop computer, all three of them arguing about how wide the man's face was. The smallest printer Marian had ever seen was set up on the desk and waiting.

The tech was Paula Dancer, the same one who'd tried to put together a composite of Rosalind Bowman's face from André Flood's unhelpful description (and ended up with a picture of herself). She looked up and saw Marian. "Hello, Lieutenant. What are you doing down here?"

"Same killer as in the Knowles case," Marian told her. "Or at least the same MO. Have you got anything?"

"I'll show you what we have so far." Dancer hit a few keys and turned the laptop so Marian could see the small screen.

"His face is narrower than that, I tell ya," one of the witnesses said, a man wearing coveralls with the name "Jerry" stitched over his heart.

The face on the screen had no mouth yet. Its most prominent feature was a hooked nose, thin and sharp-looking. Marian asked Buchanan, "You ever run across that face before?"

He said no. "I'd remember that nose."

The small room was hot and crowded, so the three detectives went outside to wait. Not too much time passed before Paula Dancer emerged carrying a stack of pictures she'd just printed out. She handed one copy each to Marian and Buchanan and gave the rest to Gloria. "They're all agreed this is pretty close, although they're not all three happy with the face width and the hairline."

The computer-generated portrait showed a clean-shaven man with black hair and eyes, the hook nose, and lips so thin they made his jaw appear more prominent than it probably was. "Naw, I don't know this guy," Buchanan repeated. "New talent in town, maybe."

Dancer pointed to the mouth. "This is unusual. Most people's lower lips are larger than the upper, but all three of the witnesses were vehement about the equal sizes here. They said he had almost no lips at all."

"This is great," Gloria said, studying the picture. "*Two* distinguishing features, nose and mouth. I'll get the pictures distributed to the bluesuits."

"We'll cover the airports," Buchanan said. "Bus and train stations too, although I'd bet this guy is used to first class. He don't know we've got his face on paper, but he could get spooked."

Gloria asked, "How many copies can that little thing you've got in there print out?"

"As many as you want," Dancer said.

"Then you take these." Gloria handed the stack of portraits to Buchanan. "I'll get more."

Marian said, "Gloria . . . discreetly?"

The other detective placed her hand over her heart. "My middle name, woman! Now I gotta get the witnesses' statements—are we done for now?"

"For now. I'll call you tomorrow."

On the way downstairs, Marian checked her watch. "You're off duty, Sergeant."

"So are you, Lieutenant."

Rush-hour traffic slowed them down. While they were waiting for a green, Buchanan said, "That Sanchez. Why won't she take the Sergeants Exam?"

Marian eased the car forward as the light changed. "Beats me. I've been after her to take it—but she always puts me off and never says why."

"I thought she was black when I first saw 'er. But with a name like Sanchez—"

"Black mother, Puerto Rican father," Marian explained. "Gloria can be black or Hispanic, as the mood takes her. You happened to catch her on one of her black days."

The minute they were back in the Midtown South stationhouse, Buchanan headed straight for the phone to get the airport watch set up. Even before taking her coat off, Marian went looking for one of the clerical workers to arrange for copies of the Knowles case reports to be delivered to Captain DiFalco.

Sergeant Campos was working late too, sitting at his desk and trying to catch up on the paperwork that constantly threatened to drown every police detective. Marian told him she needed two men from his squad to work on the Knowles case.

He objected. "We're all overloaded now. I can't dump the casework of two men on somebody else."

"I know you're overloaded and I'm sorry about this. But there's been a development." She explained about the Robin Muller shooting and the almost one hundred percent probability that it was the same shooter they were looking for in the Oliver Knowles case. "He's a hired killer with god knows how many other contracts in his pocket. We've got to stop this guy."

"Take somebody from Buchanan's squad, Lieutenant."

"I've got Buchanan himself. Now, I want two men from your squad."

"Can't the Ninth Precinct provide some manpower?"

Marian sighed. "Campos, everything I say to you, you argue with me about it. Two men. Eight o'clock tomorrow morning. My office. Got that?"

He looked disgusted, but he nodded.

Marian shucked off her coat, made a quick trip to the ladies' room, and gathered her notes together. The last thing she did before going in to report to Captain Murtaugh was call Holland and cancel their dinner date.

* 22 *

Captain Murtaugh examined the computer-generated portrait Marian had handed him. He nodded, pleased. "An easy face to spot. But no one actually saw him pull the trigger, right?"

"No one ever sees this guy pull the trigger," Marian said. "This is our man, Captain. She's alive, he sits down next to her, he stands up, she's dead. Entry wound on the left side of the chest, just as in the Knowles killing."

"You're sure she was alive when he sat down?"

"The witnesses are. They say she had to move a little to make room for him."

He nodded. "Tell me how you're handling it."

She explained the division of labor, Gloria Sanchez getting the portrait to Manhattan's bluesuits and Buchanan covering airlines and other terminals. "I'm adding two men to the Knowles investigation, now that we can go at it from both ends."

"The shooter and whoever hired him, right. I've got something else for you. The computer search turned up one other killing with the same MO. Out at Kennedy. Queens just faxed me the report."

Marian sat down and quickly read the report. The victim was a second-generation Italian named Anthony Pasquellini, a greengrocer on Mulberry Street. He'd booked passage on a TWA flight to Rome, going back for a family visit. Pasquellini was in a window seat ready to go when the pilot announced there would be a delay. Bad weather was coming in, and it would be at least two hours before they could take off. The passengers were told they could return to the terminal for that period of time if they wished.

So for two hours—actually closer to three, as it turned out—people were leaving the plane and coming back on again. Anthony Pasquellini never left his seat; the flight attendants thought he was sleeping. But one eventually began to think he "looked funny"; Pasquellini was on the corpulent side, but the attendant couldn't see his chest moving as he breathed. And his head was at a funny angle. When she tried to wake him, she discovered he was dead. The bullet wound in the left side of his chest was covered by a propped-up copy of *Opera News*.

The investigators learned that Pasquellini had been involved in a bitter feud with a rival greengrocer named Enrico Toma, a feud kept burning by personal as well as business antagonisms. Toma had an airtight alibi for the time Pasquellini was killed, and no evidence had yet been uncovered to indicate that Toma had hired a hit man. Neither Pasquellini nor Toma was connected.

Marian looked up from the report. "Not connected. Remember when the Mafia was the scariest thing around?"

Murtaugh looked grim. "Now they're just one spoke in a global network of crime."

She reread part of the report. "There's nothing before this one shooting last week?"

"Not as far back as the computerized records go. This guy has to be imported talent."

She nodded her head, thinking. "But for a stranger in

town, he sure knows how to find his way around. Robin Muller had been hiding out in Brooklyn, and he found her. This Pasquellini was on the verge of leaving the country, and he got to him in time."

"You're saying he's not imported talent?"

"No, I'm saying he must have lived here once. He may have, er, honed his skills elsewhere. Or maybe he changes his MO frequently. But he knows New York."

Murtaugh mulled that over. "That means this guy could have been here before, using a different MO each time. Hell, he could have been here a dozen times! And we'd never know it."

"It also means," Marian pointed out, "that he has a steady source of contracts here."

The captain sighed heavily, deep from the gut. "A syndicate. A ring of hired killers, operating like any other business. Right here under our noses."

"We knew from the start that was a possibility."

Suddenly Captain Murtaugh unfolded his long frame from behind his desk. "I'm getting cabin fever. Let me buy you a cardboard sandwich."

Marian welcomed the idea; her stomach was beginning to growl. They plodded downstairs to the machines and made their selections; that plus a cup of ersatz coffee was dinner. Marian leaned against the wall, chewing her dry ham-and-cheese, thinking.

She swallowed and said, "Gloria Sanchez isn't going to find any connection between Robin Muller and Oliver Knowles. The only thing they have in common is that the same man was paid to kill them both."

"Sanchez will be looking for motive?"

"She'll have to, but I don't know what she can find. Robin Muller was a schoolgirl. Not into drugs. The only thing unusual about her was this mysterious source of income she'd had for the past several months. And if she didn't even tell the guy she was living with about that, we'd be better off concentrating on the shooter and working backward."

"*If* she didn't tell the guy she was living with," Murtaugh said pointedly.

Marian tossed her empty coffee cup into the trash bin. "Yeah, I've been wondering about that. Larry Hibler—the boyfriend—wanted to make sure we understood he didn't know anything about Robin's 'job,' whatever it was."

"Bullshit. He had to know. Bring him in tomorrow," the captain ordered. "Lean on him. Get the truth out of him." He headed toward the stairs, still talking. "Make sure Sanchez does a full background check on both Muller and Hibler. And don't ease up on Knowles because now we got a shot at nailing the trigger man."

"I wasn't planning to," Marian panted, running to catch up.

The captain's long legs took the stairs two at a time. "You'll get the accountant's report on O.K. Toys tomorrow. If they're clean, forget the money motive and go after personal stuff."

She gasped a laugh. "Did you just say what I think you said?"

He stopped and turned. "Yeah, sometimes people do kill each other for reasons other than money. Or so I'm told. Larch, how many 'crimes of passion' have you investigated since you got your gold shield?"

She didn't have to think long. "Only one. But aren't all murders crimes of passion in some sense? Even this cold-blooded, hook-nosed sonuvabitch we're looking for now—he gets something out of it other than just his fee. A sense of superiority, maybe. Or perhaps the satisfaction of seeing an obstacle removed . . . like pushing a chair out of the way."

He scowled. "And you don't think that's cold-blooded?"

"To us, it is. But to him, that's his passion. Satisfaction."

Murtaugh raised an eyebrow. "Let's leave the psychological profiles to those who get paid to write them up. From you, I want hard evidence that'll stand up in court. And explanations. Like, who the hell is this Virgil?"

"I'd say he's the main man. The one who operates this ring of killers."

They were back at Murtaugh's office, but neither of them went inside. The captain leaned against the doorjamb and suggested, "It could be the code name for a contact *to* the main man."

Marian admitted the possibility. "But when Robin Muller called her boyfriend, she said that the paymaster had warned her. That sounds to me as if the paymaster is the contact and Virgil the head honcho—she said *Virgil* was going to send someone after her."

"But why would Virgil's paymaster warn one of the victims?"

"To rub it in?"

"What? I don't follow."

"Robin told her boyfriend that the paymaster had warned her 'spitefully'—that's the word she used. Isn't that odd? Spitefully. Like . . . 'Nyah, nyah, you're gonna get yours'?"

"Suggesting that the paymaster and Robin Muller had had previous contact of a not altogether satisfactory sort." Murtaugh locked eyes with Marian. "Are you thinking what I'm thinking?"

"That Robin Muller worked for Virgil?" She nodded. "It would explain a lot of things."

"Hoo." The captain leaned his head back against the doorjamb. "Where did she fit into this network of efficient killers? What was her job? This thing is like a web spreading out, with a big fat spider named Virgil sitting in the center."

"The paymaster would be closest to Virgil, wouldn't he?" she guessed.

"Seems reasonable." He straightened up. "Get that boyfriend in here. First thing tomorrow. And get the truth out of him. I don't care how you get it, but get it! You can bring out the rubber pipes, for all I care."

"Rubber hoses," she corrected with a smile.

"Pipes, hoses, whatever. But get the truth out of him!"

"I will," Marian promised.

* 23 *

She was dragging by the time she got home, four hours after her shift officially ended, bone-tired but still keyed up. She halfway hoped Holland would be waiting at her building, but he wasn't. Upstairs, she checked her answering machine; no messages.

She made herself a drink. A long shower left her feeling a little better, but she was still having trouble winding down. She went into the kitchen and opened the refrigerator—but she wasn't hungry; the undigested cardboard sandwich lay like a lump in her stomach. She thought about having another drink but didn't want one; Kelly Ingram had once told her she wasn't really a very good drinker. She picked up a book, opened it, stared at the page without seeing the words. She turned on the television and immediately turned it off again.

This was the sort of time that deep-breathing exercises to aid relaxation would help, but Marian didn't know any. She took a few experimental deep breaths. She tried holding her breath but quit as soon as it began to feel like a headache starting.

Then she turned out the lights in her living room and sat at the window, watching the street below. Wet snow was falling. Traffic was light and no pedestrians were visible on the one side of the street that Marian could see from her vantage point. She felt cooped up, trapped, imprisoned . . . but she'd been home less than an hour. It wasn't even ten o'clock yet.

After five fidgety minutes she gave up staring out the window and went to the phone. When he answered, she said simply, "Come over."

"Yes," he replied, and hung up.

It took him almost half an hour to drive crosstown and down to the less fashionable neighborhood where Marian lived. He was still ringing the bell when she opened the door.

He announced loudly, "Holland Rent-a-Stud, at your service."

She was too fatigued to rise to the bait. "Come in." He was carrying a small leather travel kit, the sort of thing women give men for Christmas when they don't know what else to buy. "What's that?"

"Necessaries. When I am summoned in the middle of the night, I expect to be offered the courtesy of a night's lodging." He held up the kit. "Toothbrush and razor."

Their lovemaking was rough and frenetic . . . just the way Marian wanted it. When they lay exhausted side by side on the rumpled bed, she began to tell him about Robin Muller and the murder-for-a-price organization that had been operating for god-knows-how-many years without the police's even catching a whiff of it. She told him about Virgil, and the paymaster, and the man with the hooked nose and thin lips. She told him about Robin Muller's probable involvement with the ring.

She said she'd thought they were through with those Murder, Incorporated, type of melodramatics. There'd always be hit men for hire, yes—but a well-organized, businesslike operation? She thought they'd stamped out that particular entrepreneurial activity for good now. They had new laws covering it. She thought she'd seen the end of that kind of stuff. Old-timey gangsterism. We kill anything for a price! Weekend specials! Group discounts!

Holland listened without interrupting. When she finally ran out of steam, he kept silent a moment longer. Then he asked, "What's bothering you so much about this case?"

"The victims," she said without hesitation. "An old man on a bus and a schoolgirl on a subway. How brave this killer is, facing such formidable opponents." She didn't try to hide her contempt. "Sneak attacks—no chance for the victims to defend themselves. Impersonal . . . killing on commission. Hit and run. Cowardly." She paused. "He's a piece of shit."

Holland said nothing but pulled her over to him.

This time their lovemaking was slow and quiet, and this time neither of them wanted to talk afterward. Marian fell asleep with her head on his shoulder. She slept the sleep of the dead.

Holland was up before she was the next morning. "A few minor details to attend to before meeting with a new client," he explained.

"Anything exciting?" Marian asked lazily, not quite ready to get up yet.

He was toweling his hair dry from the shower. "No, just another international banking concern that wants to see if I can break through their computer security."

She laughed. "That's not exciting?"

"It was once."

He started dressing. Holland was a graceful man, and she liked watching him move. "But not now?"

"Not so much. Now that I get paid for doing it, a lot of

the fun is gone. If I get caught, I won't go to prison for it. Takes the spice out of the game."

Marian tensed. She counted to five and then asked, quietly, "Why do you do that?"

"Do what?"

"Drop these little hints that you once had a sordid criminal past . . . and then never follow up, just leave me dangling."

He laughed. "Because I love to watch you go for the bait. You always do, you know."

"Is that nice? Baiting me?"

"No . . . it's rather nasty, in fact. But Marian, you absolutely *prickle* when you think you're on to something about my aforementioned sordid criminal past. You are a moralist, you know."

"A moralist!" She sat up straight in the bed. "No one has ever called me a *moralist* before!"

"They were probably afraid to. But I've never met anyone so loyal to her own sense of right and wrong as you are. It's not even a matter of belief with you. It just *is*."

"Now you're making me think of all the times I've bent the rules."

"Then they were probably bad rules—the rationalizer's favorite excuse," he said with a laugh. "Besides, we all bend the rules at one time or another. We have to."

"Like with Connie the Greek."

His playful manner vanished in an instant. Slowly he came over and stood by tne bed. "Ah. I see. You know about Connie."

"Yes." At least he was not trying to bluff his way out; she respected him for that.

A silence grew as he examined her face. "I'm not going to ask what you're going to do. You'll make your own decision without any prompting from me."

She let the silence grow a little more. "I can't do any-thing. Connie the Greek is dead. You're safe. No evidence."

A number of expressions flitted across Holland's face, too rapidly for her to read. But Marian could see him, actually see him, deciding not to ask the question he wanted to ask. He looked at his watch. "I must go. We'll speak of this another time. Or not." And he was gone.

Marian knew the question he'd wanted to ask. *What would you do about it if you did have the evidence?*

When she went into the bathroom, she found that Holland had left his toothbrush and razor there.

It was all a matter of trust.

* 24 *

Detectives Walker and Dowd were waiting in her office when she got there.

Walker and Dowd were the two who'd been lax in pursuing the suspected fence, whose name was . . . Sanderson, she remembered with an effort. She'd chewed Campos out for not overseeing the two detectives more carefully, deepening his resentment of her—but that was a different problem. "Set-back in the Sanderson case?" Marian asked.

Dowd shifted his weight. "Naw, that's all wrapped up, Lieutenant," he replied. "Sergeant Campos said you wanted two more men on the Oliver Knowles case."

And he'd sent her Walker and Dowd. Marian felt like laughing in spite of her irritation at the sergeant's perverseness. "Just let me get settled here," she said, trying to keep her face straight.

Since Dowd's desk was right outside her office door, Marian had come to know him fairly well. But Walker was a virtual stranger. A too-thin black man in his early thirties, he spoke little and always seemed to be watching. Being careful.

"Okay," she said when she had her coat off and was seated at her desk, "how are you two at leaning on people?"

"Who's the perp?" Dowd wanted to know.

"A witness, not a perp. Name of Larry Hibler. He's a student at NYU—you can get his address from Sergeant Buchanan. But there's a lot of background you'll need first. Dowd, can you bring in another chair? You'll both want to take notes."

Dowd found a chair that wasn't bolted in place and brought it into the small office. Marian closed the door and started filling them in on the Robin Muller murder as well as summarizing what they'd learned in the Oliver Knowles case. Walker's and Dowd's pens were busy getting down all the names and other data. They filled several pages of their notebooks.

While Marian was giving them their briefing, Perlmutter appeared at the door and looked in through the glass. Without missing a beat Marian pointed to her watch and held up five fingers; Perlmutter nodded and disappeared. Marian handed Walker and Dowd copies of the computer portrait of the suspected killer.

When she'd finished her briefing, Dowd shook his head. "Whew. An organization of hit men and we didn't know about it? Shit."

"Yes, hard to believe, isn't it?" Marian agreed. "But they've managed to keep under cover until now."

Walker spoke for the first time. "This new hit man—we'd better find him fast."

"Why?"

"Because he was a mistake," the detective said. "This ring has been operating for years without our tumbling to it. But the guy with the hooked nose gives it away? We'd better find him before Virgil does."

Marian thought that over. "Virgil doesn't know we know about him—at least, we don't think he does. How could he? But I suppose it's a chance we shouldn't take. All right, I'll pass the word. Now go pick up Larry Hibler. And let me know when you get back."

Walker and Dowd left. Perlmutter and O'Toole, who'd been hovering outside, came in and sat in their chairs.

Marian lifted a finger. "One phone call." She tapped out Gloria Sanchez's number at the Ninth Precinct. When Gloria came on the line, she told her they were picking up Robin Muller's boyfriend and planned to give him the grilling of his life.

"Shee-ut," Gloria said. "You beat me to it."

Aha. "You didn't believe him either?"

"At the time, I did. But I got to thinking about it later— no way he couldna known what she was doing."

"That's what we think. You're invited to the party, by the way. Come anytime."

"I'll be there. This is no single hit man we're dealing with here, is it?"

So she'd figured it out. "It looks like a whole network of them. And Gloria, when you come, could you bring along copies of your reports on the Muller shooting?" She looked at Perlmutter and O'Toole. "I've got two detectives here who're just salivating to get in on the action."

"Sure thing," Gloria said.

"Something else." Marian passed on Detective Walker's suggestion that Virgil might be looking for Hook Nose too.

O'Toole looked at Perlmutter and mouthed *Hook Nose?* The other detective just shrugged.

Gloria didn't think much of Walker's suggestion. "Hey, this has all happened too fast. The portrait's only been on the street a few hours. They don't know we know."

"Hook Nose might have been aware that he was noticed."

"And he's gonna run tell Virgil about it? Fat chance."

Marian admitted it wasn't likely. "Nevertheless, let's make this hunt highest priority."

"Honeychile, it's already double-highest-super-fuckin'-duper priority. It cain't get no higher."

"All right, then," Marian said with a laugh. "See you in a bit." She hung up.

Perlmutter inquired politely, "We're salivating to do what?"

"The Knowles killer has claimed another victim. But this time he was noticed." She pushed another copy of the portrait across the desk. "Read the reports when they get here. But now, tell me what you found at Oliver Knowles's place."

O'Toole was still staring at the portrait. "Boy, I'll know that guy if I see him!"

"A memorable face," Perlmutter agreed. "We found something, and we didn't find something," he told Marian.

"Perlmutter. It's considered bad manners to be cryptic this early in the morning. Spit it out."

"We checked through Knowles's papers at his place. Surprisingly few of them," Perlmutter said. "Checking account but no savings account. Checks were all made out to cover normal household expenses, phone bills, like that. Regular deposits of a check from O.K. Toys. That's what we found."

"So what didn't you find?"

"Cash withdrawals. There's not a single one. Yet Knowles paid for his own toys in cash, like that fancy train layout that takes up two rooms. That stuff's not cheap. But where did the cash come from?"

Marian nodded. "Unrecorded income. Okay, now we're getting somewhere. I want you to track down that accountant from the DA's office and get a preliminary report from him. Also, ask him to print out a list of the vendors O.K. Toys does business with."

O'Toole asked, "What are we going to do with that?"

"Why, you're going to call every name on the list, that's what you're going to do with it."

Perlmutter nodded. "To verify that O.K. Toys really does do business with them. They could be keeping a set of fake books that would look okay to an outside auditor."

"That's the idea," Marian agreed. She sent them on their way and closed the door behind them.

She needed to make some personal calls, now, before Walker and Dowd got back; things might get a little hectic later. Her part in making sure the wedding of Ivan Malecki and Claire Yelincic went smoothly was just about finished; she still had to find one more car for transporting members of the wedding party from the church to the banquet hall. Limousine for the bride and groom; anything that moved for everybody else. Marian was having dinner at the Yelincic house that evening, and she wanted all the details nailed down before she got there. *Like reporting to my captain,* she thought, and laughed. She got busy.

She found her last car, and was just working out the details with Claire Yelincic's second cousin once removed when a tap at the door sounded. Marian looked up to see Gloria Sanchez waiting outside—in her *latina* persona today: bright clothing, lots of jewelry and make-up. Marian wound up her conversation and waved her in.

Gloria dropped a folder on the desk. "Here are zee reports. Not much een them so far."

Marian tipped her head to the side. "'Een' them?"

Gloria grinned. "Too much, huh?"

"Hm. Where's your coat?"

"Oh, I found an empty hook out there somewhere," she said, slipping easily into her nonethnic speech pattern. "You got Larry Hibler yet?"

"No, and they should be back by now. Maybe he wasn't home."

"Then I'll wait. I'm not going back to the Ninth until Captain DiFalco's had a chance to cool off."

"What's the matter now?"

"He's pissing acid because Midtown South got the jump on him. Going after the boyfriend, I mean."

Marian was stricken, "Oh, Gloria, I got you into trouble. I'm sorry!"

But Gloria scotched that. "If it wasn't that, it'd be something else. DiFalco's jealous of Murtaugh. It's obvious as hell. And then there's you. You know what he calls you? He calls you 'my reject'. "

Marian's mouth dropped open. "I am *his* reject? When I told him I'd quit the force rather than work for *him* any longer?"

"Yeah, well, selective memory, you know. But it really pissed him to see Murtaugh take in his 'reject' and even recommend you for promotion. Just seeing you at the stationhouse last night was enough to set him off."

Marian was furious. "Oh, that ridiculous man! He turns *everything* into politics!"

Gloria smiled sadly. "Marian," she said softly, "you have a real enemy there. Be careful."

Marian pressed her lips together and nodded, grateful to Gloria for the warning.

Gloria went through some sort of mental shift and was the overstated *latina* again. "Zo. Zees Murtaugh, you like workin' for heem, yes?"

"Yes," Marian echoed, willing to change subjects. "He's helpful without being intrusive. A good boss." She wanted to add that Gloria could be working for him too if she'd take the Sergeants Exam but restrained herself.

Right then Sergeant Buchanan came up and stuck his head through the doorway. "Lieutenant, Walker and—" He broke off when he caught sight of Gloria. "Oh, sorry, didn't know you had somebody in here."

"It's all right," Marian said. "Come on in."

"'Allo!" Gloria trilled.

Buchanan stepped into the office and squinted his eyes. "Sanchez? Is that you?"

"*Sí!*"

"No shit. God, I didn't know you!"

Gloria flashed her eyes. "Zat's zee idea, beeg boy."

Buchanan got a kick out of that. "Call me Buck."

Marian sighed; he'd never told *her* to call him Buck. "You have something to tell me, Buchanan?"

He was all business again. "Walker and Dowd are back with Larry Hibler. They have him in interrogation room three."

"Then let's go," Marian said.

* 25 *

Larry Hibler was proving a tougher nut to crack than Marian had thought. Robin Muller's boyfriend looked like a scared kid, in over his head and not knowing what to do about it. But he was sticking to his story that he didn't know anything about Robin's job.

Captain Murtaugh stood behind the one-way glass with Marian and Gloria Sanchez, watching Walker and Dowd work the witness. Gloria and Buchanan had already spelled them once, and now they were back for a second go. They were observing the letter of the law, but just barely. When Hibler said he needed the men's room, Walker and Dowd had let him squirm until he'd asked four times. When he hoarsely requested a drink of water, they let him get a little thirstier before bringing him one.

"That kid's hiding something," Murtaugh muttered. "It's as plain as the nose on your face. Damn! The more he delays telling us, the more he increases our chances of losing the trail."

Marian raised an eyebrow. "Rubber hose?"

"Don't tempt me."

They watched a little longer. Gloria Sanchez said, "They're getting close. He's not gonna hold out much longer."

"I hope you're right," Murtaugh said. "Keep me posted." He left.

Walker and Dowd had an interesting technique. It wasn't good cop/bad cop; it was more like sophisticate/oaf. Walker was the sophisticate, using long words and increasingly complex sentences, his tone measured and reasonable. Dowd had turned into an angry street tough, the kind that can't get through a sentence without saying *fucking* at least once. Not surprisingly, it was Walker that Hibler was responding to, actually edging away from Dowd and his loud, abrasive voice.

"Want me to go out and get us some lunch?" Gloria asked.

"Oh, that would be great," Marian said, thinking of last night's cardboard-sandwich supper.

Detective O'Toole opened the door of their observation cubicle, a huge grin on his face. "Lieutenant?"

"You've got something." Marian felt a stab of anticipation.

"Oh boy, have we!"

The two women stepped out into the hallway and closed the door to the little room. "What?" Marian asked.

"The vendors we've been calling."

"O.K. Toys did not do business with them?"

"They're phonies," O'Toole said excitedly. "Not one of the suppliers O.K. Toys says they're doing business with even exists! Sham, fake, make-believe. The whole thing is a front!"

Marian raised two fists over her head. "Yessss! Now we got them. Where's Perlmutter?"

"In the squadroom."

"O.K. Toys?" Gloria Sanchez asked.

Marian let O'Toole fill her in as they hurried back to the squadroom. Perlmutter was just hanging up the phone as they reached his desk. "The accountant says they have invoices to back up every transaction they've got listed on the books. You know what they did, don't you? They had a bunch of business forms printed up, different phony vendors, and just made out the invoices to themselves. It's all a big scam to keep the IRS satisfied. The feds aren't going to check any further than the invoices."

"And they've been getting away with it for years," Marian said in amazement.

"Pick up David Unger?" O'Toole asked.

"Oh, yes, indeedy. I'll have the warrant by the time you get back. If he wants his lawyer, pick him up too. He had to have been in on the scam himself."

"Elmore Zook," O'Toole added for Gloria's benefit.

"What about Austin Knowles?" Perlmutter asked.

Marian said no. "He had nothing to do with the running of the toy company—that was his daddy's bailiwick. If we can prove he had guilty knowledge of what was going on, we can pick him up later. But for now, leave him alone. Okay . . . let's go."

The next few hours moved like lightning. The attorney from the DA's office said he was calling in a federal prosecutor, that the charge against Unger would be tax fraud. He complained that the police still hadn't linked Unger to the hit man who killed Oliver Knowles. Marian assured him they were getting to that.

She ate the lunch that Gloria brought her at her desk, barely tasting the food. Gloria had then gone back to her own precinct, asking to be notified if Larry Hibler decided to talk. The federal prosecutor showed up trailing two IRS accountants; they insisted on double-checking all the vendors on the O.K. Toys list. Marian herself had a short and unsatisfying interview with David Unger.

She managed a few minutes with him before Elmore Zook showed up. One bluesuit was in the interrogation room with them, Unger's guard. "We've got you cold," she told Unger. "There's no way in the world you can explain away these phony records."

"I'm not saying anything until my lawyer gets here," Unger replied. He sat there so stolidly—a good-looking, prosperous man putting up with the foolishness of the police. Determined to be civilized about it.

"What were you doing, laundering money? For whom?"

No answer.

"Look, Unger," she said, "we know this whole thing was set up by Oliver Knowles. You just inherited it. Where did the money come from?"

"I'm not making a statement without my lawyer."

"Uh-huh, well, we may just be charging your lawyer as well. If it comes to a choice between saving his own skin or yours, which one do you think he'll choose?"

No reply.

"One of you arranged the hit on Oliver Knowles. Why? He was out of the game. Why'd you have to get rid of him?"

Stony silence.

"Unger, don't you understand? This tax fraud charge is just to hold you until we get one or two more pieces of evidence. We *are* going to charge you with murder."

The first sign of nervousness: he started playing with his mustache. "I want my lawyer."

It went on like that a couple of minutes more, until Elmore Zook came bursting into the room, radiating a sense of outrage that Marian didn't think was faked. The first thing he did was call her a meddlesome bitch.

"Who do you think you are?" Zook demanded. "Some jumped-up little nobody making trouble for respectable businessmen! David Unger worked all his life for what he's got . . . and you come along with a badge handed to you under some half-assed quota system and you think you have the right—you actually think you have the *right*—to harass a man like David Unger!"

The veneer of courtesy Zook had displayed at their previous meeting was proving pretty thin. The older man was breathing heavily, more angry at the situation than intimidated by it. The bluesuit guarding Unger slowly closed the door, glowering at Zook. "The phony books," Marian said evenly. "How does your respectable businessman explain that?"

"Don't say anything, Dave," Zook warned his client unnecessarily. "We don't have to explain anything to you, Miss Know-It-All. Tax fraud is a federal matter—we'll clear up this misunderstanding with the federal prosecutor. The police have nothing to do with it. Go home, you silly broad. Leave the running of the world to the men who know how to do it."

Surprisingly, the bluesuit spoke up. "Hey, don't talk to the lieutenant like that, you!" Zook didn't even acknowledge him. Marian was puzzled by the lawyer's strategy. Did he think he could *insult* her into dropping the case?

Unger made an attention-catching noise. "She says she's going to charge me with Oliver's murder."

Zook hit the ceiling. "Of all the crazy, incompetent . . . are you ready to charge him right now? Because if you aren't, he's walking."

"No, he isn't. A federal prosecutor and the IRS are in this building right now, and we're holding Unger for them to question. Your client's not going anywhere, Mr. Zook. Except to prison."

Zook stared at her murderously for a long moment;

Marian stared back, unflinching. Zook turned to his client and said, "Don't say anything, Dave, not a single word. I'll get you out of here." He charged out of the interrogation room, even more angry than when he'd come in.

Marian smiled coldly at Unger. "Well. That was helpful."

Unger followed instructions, said nothing.

"Zook won't have to 'get you out of here.' You'll be released once the feds have finished questioning you, until they're ready to bring charges. But you can kiss O.K. Toys goodbye. And Unger—no sudden trips out of town. Got that?"

He didn't answer.

She watched him playing with his mustache and wished for some sort of insight into the man. She didn't know David Unger—what he watched on TV, whether he was good to his family, what he liked to eat, what he did in his spare time. The man was a cipher. She'd get Perlmutter and O'Toole to dig a little deeper. But Unger wasn't going to tell her anything about himself. Not ever. Marian motioned to the bluesuit to take him away.

Murtaugh had been observing through the one-way glass. He met Marian in the hallway and said, "You didn't expect them *not* to play hardball, did you?"

Marian shook her head. "No, but it was the wrong guy who was playing. Unger seems so . . . mild. I can see Zook ordering the hit, but not Unger."

"Yep, it's a pretty good routine they've got worked out," the captain replied indifferently.

"You think it's an act?"

"In this place," Murtaugh said, "everything's an act."

"You know, there's one possibility we've never really considered. Maybe Oliver Knowles was exactly what he appeared to be—a nice old man who spent his life making toys. And maybe his company wasn't turned into a money-laundering front until after he retired and was no longer involved in the day-to-day operation of the business. Then somehow Knowles found out what Unger was doing."

Murtaugh was nodding. "And that's why Knowles had to be killed . . . to protect the scam. It would have to be a pretty new scam, then—only a few years, however long since Knowles retired. And Unger set it all up."

Marian was trying not to get her hopes up prematurely, but they had Virgil in a pincer movement. They knew what one of his shooters looked like, and they knew who one of his clients was. Hook Nose or Unger, either one could lead them to the man who dispensed death as if it were any other service available for a fee. Marian couldn't think of anything she wanted more than to put that sonuvabitch out of business forever.

Then at a little before four, only a matter of minutes until Marian's shift was supposed to end, Larry Hibler finally broke.

* 26 *

Robin Muller had been a courier, Larry Hibler said.

The job had been simplicity itself. In the mail would come an envelope with no return address. Inside would be a locker key taped to an index card on which was written the location of the locker. Sometimes Robin would have to go as far as one of the airports to find the locker.

Inside the locker was always the same thing: a large manila envelope with a sheet of instructions clipped to the outside that told where the envelope was to be delivered. It was always a public place—a park, a restaurant, a movie theater, a hotel lobby. But a different place every time.

Did she always deliver the envelope to the same person?

Not always. Robin could tell if it would be someone she'd not delivered to before because the instructions would say give the envelope to the man wearing the green plaid muffler or the woman carrying a certain book; there was always some specific means of identifying them.

Woman?

One woman. The rest were men. Robin never knew their names. After she'd delivered the envelope, Robin would go to a second address listed on the instruction sheet. Again, it was always a public place and never the same place twice.

There the paymaster would hand her a small envelope containing her fee, in cash.

Who's this paymaster?

Robin never knew his name, but he knew hers. And where she lived. The first time she'd met him to be paid, she'd had to show him some ID before he'd hand over the envelope. He'd known what name to check for. Thereafter, their meetings had been silent ones, except for times when he complained that she was late.

What does he look like?

Hibler had no idea; he'd never seen the man and Robin had never described him. All she'd said about him was that he gave her the creeps. Oh, wait—she did say he wore an overcoat that was a nauseating mustard color. She'd never seen a man's coat in that particular shade before.

Did Robin ever look inside these manila envelopes that she delivered?

She was afraid to. She'd been warned not to look, and there was also a wax seal on the back. Everyone she'd delivered to always checked the seal before accepting the envelope. She suspected they'd been instructed not to take it if the seal was broken.

What did she *think* she was delivering?

They'd talked about that, Hibler said. He'd thought she was delivering drug money, but Robin had said nobody would trust the delivery of money to an unbonded stranger. Besides, the envelopes were flat. No, they were just papers of some sort. She couldn't even begin to guess what.

How did she get this courier job?

Virgil called her. Robin never met him; it was all done over the phone. She was looking for part-time work. She'd been asking around, posting on bulletin boards—both electronic and the old-fashioned kind. Virgil could have gotten her name anywhere.

Didn't it occur to her that she was involved in something illegal?

Yes, but the money was so good! Robin had been paid three hundred dollars for each delivery; sometimes the job took only a couple of hours, depending on where the locker with the envelope was located. And since she was paid in cash, there was no tax to worry about. To a graduate student trying to live on a scholarship, the job was manna from heaven.

So, Larry, what went wrong? Why was she killed?

The only reason he could think of, he said, was that she'd missed a couple of deliveries. The first time, she'd lost the locker key and couldn't pick up the envelope. The second time, she'd overslept. Robin had pulled an all-nighter, studying for an eleven A.M. exam. After the exam she'd gone back to their apartment for a nap; she'd either slept through the alarm or forgot to set it, because she woke up past the time she was supposed to make the delivery. She'd hurried to the locker to get the envelope, but it was gone. Did people really get killed over things like that? Hibler wondered. What kind of man was this Virgil?

"A very evil one," Sergeant Buchanan said. "When you first reported her missin', you didn't say nothin' to me about her workin' as a courier. But you did drop hints that there was somethin' shady about her new source of income. Why'd you do that?"

Hibler's haggard face turned away from the sergeant. "I was afraid you'd think she'd just walked out on me. I figured if you thought something funny was going on, you'd really look for her."

Buchanan sat back in his chair, satisfied. Detective Walker asked, "How often did Robin make these deliveries?"

"It was very irregular," Hibler said. "One week she made three deliveries. Another time she went two weeks without making any."

"Did Virgil ever call again after that first time he hired her?"

"I don't think so. She never mentioned another call."

Walker nodded to his partner. Dowd got up and went into the adjoining room, on the other side of the one-way glass. "Anything else?"

The little room was crowded. Buchanan's phone call to the Ninth Precinct had caught Gloria Sanchez just as she was leaving. Marian and Captain Murtaugh, as well as Perlmutter and O'Toole, had all been listening.

Gloria said bluntly, "You're gonna have to tell him." The Hispanic lilt was gone from her voice.

"Tell him what?" Dowd asked. "That his girlfriend was delivering instructions to hit men? Sanchez, he'd be outa here so fast you wouldn't even know he'd been here."

"So what?" Gloria retorted. "We got everything he can tell us. And maybe he oughta get outa here. *Way* outa here. Like Tibet."

"She's right," Marian said. "He has a right to know what Robin was involved in."

"Get him to sign his statement," Captain Murtaugh instructed. "*Then* tell him."

Dowd grunted and left to take care of it.

The others followed him out, glad to be free of the confining little room. "Conference," Murtaugh said.

A change in shift had taken place during the interrogation; the squadroom was filled with night staff just coming on duty. Murtaugh's office couldn't hold more than three or four people comfortably, and Marian's was smaller still. Marian sent O'Toole to fetch Walker and Dowd; they all trooped downstairs to the briefing room, where the patrol cops were given their instructions every day at roll call.

One captain, one lieutenant, one sergeant, and five detectives clustered around the chalkboard at the head of the room. The captain said, "Lieutenant, draw us a picture."

Marian stepped up to the chalkboard. "It's shaping up to look like this." She wrote:

client → ? → Virgil → paymaster → courier → shooter

"Hook Nose at one end of the chain, David Unger at the other. We don't know how the client makes contact with Virgil. But imagine more chains radiating out from the paymaster, one for each courier he pays off. And we can't assume that Virgil has only one paymaster. You can get an idea from that how big this thing is."

Perlmutter said, "Only one buffer between the client and Virgil? I'll bet there's more than that."

"Hm, that's probably right." Marian added a second question mark between "Virgil" and "client." "There could be a half dozen there."

"A chain is as strong as its weakest link," Buchanan pronounced sententiously. "And Robin Muller was the weak link. So what's Virgil gonna do? Put in a stronger link."

"What are you getting at, Buck?" Murtaugh asked.

"Send a female undercover. She could pose as a graduate student, ask around about part-time work the way Muller did."

"And get killed the way Muller did." Murtaugh shook his head. "Too dangerous."

Marian said, "Virgil's already got a replacement, I'd bet

on it. The guy's just too organized to leave a gap of any kind in his network. Any other suggestions?"

"Find Hook Nose," said Gloria Sanchez.

They all nodded. "That's the way we're going to get him," Dowd said. "Through that end of the chain."

"This client, David Unger," Walker asked. "What's the story there?"

"He's not talking," Marian replied. "And he's not going to, unless we find a way to link him to Virgil. Probably not even then. We'll have a better chance of cutting a deal with Hook Nose, once we find him."

"If we find him."

"We'll find him," Murtaugh said positively. "It's only a matter of time. All right, let's all sleep on it. This has been a good day's work, everyone. Now go home."

Perlmutter looked at his watch. "My wife's going to kill me."

Marian said, "Walker, Dowd." They turned. "That was good work, in the interrogation."

Dowd tried not to look pleased at the compliment. Walker said, "Thanks, Lieutenant." They left along with the others; Dowd was asking Gloria Sanchez to come have a drink with him.

"You too, Larch," Murtaugh said with a smile. "You've put in a long week. Go out, have dinner, have some fun."

"Dinner!" Marian said, horrified. She checked the time. "I'm supposed to be in Queens in twenty minutes!"

"Good luck!" he called after her running figure.

27

Marian had called from her car to say she'd be a few minutes late, so Mrs. Aphra Yelincic was still smiling by the time she got there. Dinner had gone smoothly. At first Marian had had difficulty making the mental shift from Virgil to small talk; but Mrs. Yelincic had helped enormously by grilling her on whether or not she missed making a home for a husband and children. Claire Yelincic had tried to divert her mother's inquisitiveness to a different subject, but Ivan Malecki hadn't lifted a finger; he'd sat there grinning at her the whole time Mrs. Yelincic was poking and prying. Mr. Yelincic had nodded and smiled.

After dinner they'd once again gone over Marian's responsibilities as best man. Everything was taken care of that could be taken care of before the day of the wedding itself, which was the coming Thursday. Mrs. Yelincic warned Marian at least four times that she'd need to remind the ushers what time the rehearsal started Wednesday evening.

Marian's invitation was for herself "and guest." "So who're you bringing?" Ivan wanted to know.

"Probably Holland. If we're still speaking."

Ivan snorted. "Better get a back-up."

"Who's Holland?" Claire asked.

"Marian's on-again, off-again boyfriend."

Marian had to smile at the thought of how Holland would react to hearing himself called a *boyfriend*.

"What is Mr. Holland's first name?" Mrs. Yelincic asked Marian sweetly.

"Curt."

"And he is," Ivan said with a nod.

"And what does Mr. Curt Holland do for a living?" Mrs. Yelincic continued.

Next she'll be asking me if his intentions are honorable. "He's a private investigator—runs his own agency. He used to be with the FBI."

The older woman's face lit up. "An FBI man!"

"Former FBI. Very former. Holland hates the FBI."

Unexpectedly, Mr. Yelincic said, "Oh, that's too bad." Everyone looked at him. He quickly retreated to nod-and-smile.

Mrs. Yelincic was not to be diverted. "And what are your plans with Mr. Curt Holland?"

Marian smiled. "To get him to come to the wedding. Beyond that, no plans."

That was not the answer the older woman wanted to hear. "Please don't take this the wrong way, Marian, dear—but you're not getting any younger, you know." Claire groaned. "If you are serious about Mr. Holland," Mrs. Yelincic went on, "you really mustn't delay much longer. So long as you're sure he would make a suitable husband."

Ivan sniggered. "Oh, he suits her all right!"

"Ivan!" Mrs. Yelincic remonstrated. "You mustn't make personal remarks. It's not polite." She looked surprised when everyone burst out laughing.

Claire said, "Kelly Ingram sent an acceptance. Can you imagine? Kelly Ingram! At *my* wedding!"

"Hey, I'll be there too," Ivan teased.

Marian listened to their cheerful chatter and felt herself relaxing from the day's tensions. Mrs. Yelincic was a wonderful throwback, the kind of professional mother you didn't much see anymore, thank goodness. But Marian was able to like the woman, because she knew she wouldn't have any sustained contact with her. She would *not* like having her for a mother-in-law. But Ivan seemed to have no problem with the prospect; he kidded Mrs. Yelincic and took no offense at her ways. It would be all right.

When the evening drew to an end, Marian's thanks were sincere; she'd enjoyed the hominess of the scene. She left with one last warning ringing in her ears about reminding the ushers of the rehearsal Wednesday evening.

At home she got ready for bed feeling bone-tired . . . but it was the good kind of tiredness, the kind that would let her sleep. She crawled into bed thinking of Holland. The last two nights, she had shared a bed with him. She felt a little sad that he wasn't there now.

The phone rang.

"Tomorrow?" he asked.

"Yes," she said. "Oh yes."

"When?"

She concentrated. "Noon. Do you mind coming by the stationhouse?"

"I'll be there."

She heard the click as he hung up.

Saturday was not one of her workdays, but Marian couldn't stay away from the station after yesterday's breakthroughs. No sign of Hook Nose yet, but the word had been sent out to double the effort to find him. Marian had one bad moment when she saw Captain DiFalco walking through the detectives' squadroom at Midtown South; but he was there to see Murtaugh, not her. A lot of brass around for a Saturday morning.

Oddly, DiFalco didn't stay long. And when he left, he was clearly in a hurry to get out of the place. Marian shrugged and turned to a pile of reports she hadn't had time to read yesterday. But before she could get started, Captain Murtaugh loomed in her doorway.

"I just got a call from the Commissioner's office," he said. "I'm to report immediately and explain why we've not yet caught this hired killer who's quote running rampant through the city unquote."

"Oh boy."

"The Commissioner himself is coming in to hear what I have to say." He gave her an ironic grin. "Your former captain was in my office when the call came. I suggested that since this was now a joint Midtown South/Ninth Precinct investigation, he might wish to accompany me to the Commissioner's office. DiFalco declined."

Marian gave a short laugh. "Why does that not surprise me?"

"I suppose it's too much to hope for, but if anything comes in about Hook Nose while I'm there—let me know immediately."

She said she would. He left; Marian had noticed that he didn't appear anxious about the upcoming interview. She supposed that yesterday's breakthroughs would be enough to convince the Powers That Be that the police were on top of the investigation. She turned back to the reports.

Most of them were from Campos's squad; Buchanan's was a little behind because of the sergeant's involvement with the Robin Muller case. Police detectives were always behind in their reports. Marian had been in the same position long enough herself to know what it was like, trying to keep up with all the paperwork. If the sergeants in charge of the squads didn't keep after the detectives, some of those reports never would get written.

Two hours later Marian had finished the reports and Captain Murtaugh was back; he gave her the okay signal on his way to his office. It was eleven-thirty. Holland wouldn't be there for another half hour. She might as well wait for him downstairs, save him the trouble of getting a visitor's pass.

But at the head of the stairs she veered and went to Murtaugh's office instead. He looked up when he saw her standing in the doorway.

"We're putting all our eggs in one basket," she said.

He knew what she meant. "Gambling everything on picking up Hook Nose. What else can we do if David Unger is a dead end? He's not going to incriminate himself."

"I'm putting Perlmutter and O'Toole on a deep background check Monday. Everything they can find about Unger. Tax fraud isn't good enough—the man ordered a murder. There must be some way we can link him to Virgil."

"I'm open to suggestion."

Marian had half an idea, not completely worked out. "Whatever O.K. Toys is a front for, it was Oliver Knowles who set it up, not Dave Unger. So our kindly little old toymaker was a criminal. Do you think it's likely that the toymaker's son never knew what Daddy was doing?"

"Austin Knowles?" Murtaugh chewed that over. "Get him for guilty knowledge?"

"Austin must be ready to jump at the chance to put away the man who killed his father. Offer him immunity in exchange for spilling the beans about what was really going on behind that toy company front."

"That would help the feds' tax fraud case, not our murder case."

"Maybe, but it's the only cage we've got to rattle. There's a chance Austin knows something that will let us link Dave Unger to Virgil."

The captain thought it over, and then decided. "All right, go for it. But check with the DA's office Monday about immunity before you approach Austin Knowles."

"Right. Thanks, Captain." She turned to leave and almost walked into Holland.

"Yes, I'm early," he said. He looked coolly at Murtaugh and said nothing.

But Murtaugh did. One word. "Holland."

Holland nodded. "Murtaugh."

Murtaugh roused himself to further effort. "I understand we owe you thanks for doing the computer work tracing our missing Rosalind Bowman."

"You understand incorrectly. You owe me nothing."

The captain glared but kept his civil tone. "Nevertheless, I do thank you for helping the police."

"You're welcome," Holland said icily. "Your gratitude means a great deal to me."

"I had a feeling it would." Murtaugh now matched Holland's iciness.

"How reassuring, to learn your 'feeling' is so reliable." Holland smiled a slow, sarcastic smile. "That must be a great comfort to you."

Murtaugh's face was glacial. "More than you can possibly know."

Impasse.

Both men looked away, toward Marian. "Don't look at me," she said blandly. "I'm not going to smooth things over for you. You got yourselves into this, you can get yourselves out."

It was Murtaugh who laughed. "Go on, go. I'll see you Monday."

On the stairway down, Marian fretted. "Why don't you and the captain get along? I know why he doesn't like you—you're rude and arrogant every time you speak to him. But why don't you like him?"

"Because he's not rude and arrogant," Holland answered blithely. "Now, where would you like to go for lunch?"

* 28 *

They managed to avoid the point of contention between them all through lunch. Afterward, neither of them wanted to go anywhere. The weather was foul; the moisture falling from the sky had stopped pretending to be snow and was coming down in a cold, steady drizzle. They ended up in Holland's apartment.

Marian stood at the glass sliding door that led to the balcony, looking out over a gray Central Park. A rainy Saturday afternoon ought to be the perfect time for a good snuggle, she thought unhappily. Yet they could barely talk to each other, tiptoeing around the subject as if it were a bomb.

She decided to bring it out into the open; they were too old to be playing Let's Pretend. Without turning around from the glass door, she said, "You obtained an investigator's license through fraudulent means. That's a felony."

He came up to stand behind her but didn't touch her. "I did take the state licensing exam."

And probably aced it, she thought. "You have too much money. You've always had too much money." She turned to face him. "Look at this place," gesturing vaguely to the posh apartment. "Your offices . . . they scream money, money, money. Where does it come from, Holland? Where do you get *all this money?*"

"I earn it," he said shortly.

She just looked at him. "That's the kind of answer you always give me. Abrupt, unresponsive. You're the most secretive man I've ever known. I don't know anything about you, I don't even know where you were born—I don't know what kind of life you lived before I met you."

"London."

"What?"

"I was born in London."

That surprised her. "You're British?"

"I'm an American citizen."

Hm. "Your parents are American?"

"I don't know who my parents were."

Oh, good heavens. "Have you tried to find them?"

"No."

The way he said it made it clear the matter held no interest for him, speaking of them in the past tense as if they were dead. Whoever they were who gave him life—they weren't part of that life. Subject closed.

He turned away and started pacing. "If I'm secretive, it's because certain things are best kept secret. For my own self-protection. I admit I have done things that you would say I should not have done. I've skirted the law more than once. But that was a different life. I'm not living that life now." He stopped and faced her. "Can't that be enough, Marian? Can't you accept me for my present life alone? For what I *am*?"

"Holland—"

"I'm not hurting anyone. I'm not robbing any banks or running any frauds. I've opened a business, my first ever. I've assumed responsibility for nine employees now, with more to come later. For all of my life, I've never called any place in the world home—but now I'm trying to anchor myself to one spot. Here. Can't that be enough?"

Could it? He was angry, proud. He was telling her there were things about his life he'd not reveal to her or anyone, that some part of him would always remain private. She'd never know the total man. The question then became: Would the part of him he was willing to share suffice for her? Could she live knowing she would never know?

She looked at that tense face waiting for her reply. "Then I guess it will have to be enough," she said quietly.

Holland moved swiftly toward her and wrapped both arms around her, holding her close. They stood like that a long time, until the tension had drained out of him and was replaced by something very like joy. He said, "You know, I'd stopped looking for you."

"For me?"

"For a partner. For someone I belonged with."

In the bedroom they set about celebrating their new understanding. For the truth was, Marian was happy when she was with Holland. Maybe she too had stopped looking for a partner, and he was as big a surprise to her as she was to him. She felt a grudging admiration for his refusal to spill his guts for her. This was a private man she had here; his air of reserve was not a challenge, but something to be respected. She knew she already had that same respect from him. In spite of all the baggage he brought with him, Holland was the one she belonged with.

They lazed the afternoon away, making slow, quiet love and reveling in their new freedom from tension. It was something like being let out of prison. They talked a little and laughed a little, at peace with each other.

On the table on Marian's side of the bed, her beeper sounded.

"I knew it was too good to last," Holland said. He picked up the phone receiver from the table on his side and pulled up the antenna. "I don't suppose you could be persuaded to tell them you're in the hospital having your appendix removed?"

"Gimme." She took the receiver and punched in the number of Midtown South.

The police dispatcher told her there was an intruder at the Broadhurst Theatre, a young woman who'd been lying in wait for Kelly Ingram. When Ms Ingram tried to throw her out, the intruder escaped—and was hiding in the theater right now. The stage manager didn't want police tramping all over the place looking for her during the matinée performance, so she was still there. Since the lieutenant was a friend of Ms Ingram's, the dispatcher thought she'd want to know.

Marian thanked the dispatcher for informing her and broke the connection. She told Holland what was going on and asked if he'd like to go to the Broadhurst with her. "I'm not on duty. We'd be dropping in as Kelly's friends."

"Of course I'll go," he said. "Kelly's being stalked?"

"Technically, no. This woman has never menaced Kelly or interfered with what she was doing. She's just always hanging around. A nuisance, not a threat. This is the first time she's ever invaded the theater. I wonder if she broke into Kelly's dressing room? If she did, then we've got something to charge her with."

It was dark outside; they'd lingered longer than they thought. By the time they were showered and dressed and had taken a cab to the Broadhurst, the rest period between the matinee and evening performances was over; Kelly was onstage performing again. Two uniformed officers were stationed backstage, looking very much out of place.

Marian didn't know either of them. She went up to the nearest and identified herself and led him to the dressing rooms section where they could talk. Holland wandered off in search of the stage manager.

The officer, whose name was Franzino, said he and his partner had searched for the intruder between performances as well as they could. "Sure is a lot of places to hide in a theater," he said ruefully. "We couldn't cover everything. The stage manager, he don't want us moving around during the performance. So we have to wait 'til they're done."

"Are there just the two of you?"

"Yeah. Well, this intruder ain't armed or dangerous. We catch her, it's just a trespassing charge. It's no big deal, Lieutenant."

"Maybe. Was she hiding in Kelly Ingram's dressing room?"

"Nope. Kelly Ingram, she said she unlocked the door to her dressing room and before she could get it closed again, this Banner woman had slipped inside. No breaking and entering."

"Hm. And you're going to resume your search after the performance? What if Banner just walks out with the audience?"

"We got a good description, Lieutenant. Me and my partner'll be out front watching the audience when they leave. The doorkeeper's gonna watch the backstage exit."

Marian nodded; it was as good an arrangement as possible with only two bluesuits on duty. She warned Officer Franzino that Banner was kind of nondescript and easy to overlook.

Back near the stage area, she caught sight of Holland standing in the wings watching the play.

When she went up to him, he put his mouth close to her ear and said, low, "Leo Gunn knows this Carla Banner. She once worked for him, as an assistant stage manager."

That was interesting. So Carla the Mouse had once tried

for a theatrical career herself . . . and failed? And was now trying to live her life vicariously through Kelly?

The first act of *The Apostrophe Thief* drew to an end. Kelly came storming off the stage, spotted Marian, and marched right up to her. "I want you to explain to me," she said heatedly, "exactly what is considered justifiable homicide in this state!"

Marian smiled. "You won't have to kill her. We'll get her."

"I hope so," Kelly retorted. "Because if you don't . . . I will."

* 29 *

Carla Banner had stayed in the theater all night, she'd told Kelly. She'd bought a ticket for Friday night, watched the play, and then hidden while the rest of the audience filed out after the performance. It was the only way she could think of to get to Kelly alone.

And why? She wanted to be Kelly's right hand, she'd said. She wanted to persuade the star to let her take care of her. She'd make Kelly's appointments, answer her fan mail, arrange her transportation, fetch and carry . . . whatever Kelly needed to be done, she'd do it. She wanted to take care of all those troublesome little details that clutter up a life, leaving Kelly free to concentrate on her career.

"She wants me to grow dependent on her, that's what she wants," Kelly grumbled. "She kept saying, 'You *need* me—I wish I could make you understand how much you *need* me.'" Kelly snorted. "I need Carla Banner in my life the way I need a hole in the head."

"Obviously she's the one with the need," Holland remarked dryly. "This one isn't going to go away just because you tell her to."

"So what do I do? How do I get rid of her?"

"Your mistake," Ian Cavanaugh said, "was in being too

nice to her in the first place. You must never let a fan start thinking of you as a personal friend."

They were in the big brownstone that Ian shared with Abigail James. The playwright was still in Hollywood, still submitting to that particular brand of California torture called the story conference. Ian hadn't wanted to go out to eat because he was expecting a call from Abby, so they were all sitting in the dining room around a munificent deli spread. Ian brought a phone in from another room and plugged it in.

Marian swallowed a bite of her food and said, "Carla Banner must have family. Maybe they could make her see the error of her ways. Worth a try."

"Do you know," Ian said, "that name sounds so familiar to me. I know I've heard it before. Carla Banner."

Holland said, "She was once Leo Gunn's assistant."

"Oh, is that right?" Ian closed his eyes to concentrate, opened them again. "No, I can't place her."

Holland was doing all his eating with his right hand. He'd pulled his chair closer to Marian's and was resting his left hand lightly on the back of her chair. Not really possessive, not really warning Ian Cavanaugh off—but some sort of gesture was being made. Marian smiled to herself; Holland still had a few old bugaboos to get rid of himself.

Kelly poured herself another drink; she'd barely touched her food. "How could she get out of the theater without being seen? Two cops watching out front, and she slipped by right under their noses."

Carla Banner wasn't in the theater, so that's what must have happened. Marian regarded her friend closely; Kelly was truly worried. "Kel," she said, "they had only a description to go on. But think what happened there tonight. Carla was being *hunted by the police*. Do you have any idea how terrifying that can be? Knowing that the cops are after *you*? She sees herself as a complete innocent, I'm sure, which would make it all the more frightening when men in uniform carrying guns come looking for her."

Kelly slowly put down her drink. "You mean she may have been scared off?"

"I think it's quite likely. Here's a young woman who so desperately wants to belong that she loses all sense of judgement. She's fixated on you, and that makes her do things that wouldn't even occur to people who live normal lives. But Carla doesn't have any life except you."

"Oh, god."

"But that's *her* doing, not yours. It's her responsibility. And maybe being chased by the police just might force her to face up to what she's doing. She's bound to be shaken by what happened."

Kelly was visibly perking up. "Then tonight might be a *good* thing."

"Wouldn't surprise me in the least."

Kelly turned to her co-star. "Hear that, Ian? I might just be rid of the pest!"

"A toast," Ian responded. "To freedom from importunate fans everywhere!" They clicked glasses.

"Very nicely done," Holland murmured into Marian's ear.

"Is 'importunate' a real word," Kelly asked Ian, "or did you just make that up?"

Marian had simply wanted to relieve her friend's mind; but she could only hope that Carla Banner would be scared off. She hadn't mentioned the other possibility, that tonight's police hunt would turn Banner against Kelly—and change her from nuisance to threat. It didn't seem likely, but it could happen.

"Of course it's a real word," said Ian, pretending huffiness. "I never make up words. That's Abby's job." On cue, the telephone rang. "And there she is!"

Ian answered, and told Abby who else was there and that he was putting her on the speakerphone. But before anyone else could even say hello, he demanded, "Just exactly *when* are you coming home?"

They could hear her sigh all the way from California. "I was hoping to leave tomorrow, but I'd better stay on a few more days. End of next week, I think, Ian."

He grumbled. "You said that last week."

"I know. It can't be helped."

Kelly spoke up. "Abby, *wait* 'til you hear what happened tonight!" She went on to tell her all about Carla Banner and how the police had come to the theater but hadn't been able to find her. When she finished, the phone remained silent. "Abby?"

"I'm here. My god. Carla Banner."

"Aha!" said Ian. "You know the name too! Who is she?"

"We've both worked with her, Ian," Abby said. "She was Leo's assistant stage manager on *Foxfire*."

His face changed. "*Foxfire*. I remember her now. She quit right before a performance."

"She didn't have much choice," Abby's voice said dryly. "Her father came and dragged her out. Kelly, do you mean that that mousy little girl is the one who's been dogging you?"

"That's the one."

"Carla Banner. I haven't thought about her in years."

Ian said, "Well, she's not exactly memorable, is she? And that seems to be her problem."

"I suppose," Abby said. Her voice brightened. "Who else is there—Marian?"

"Hi, Abby," Marian said. "How's Hollywood?"

"Oh, same as always," the playwright said. "Filled with shallow, underinformed people making decisions involving literally millions of dollars. And the things they want to do to *The Apostrophe Thief*—Kelly, at one point they were actually talking about sending you over a waterfall in a canoe."

"*What?*" Kelly screeched.

"Wa-ter-fall?" Ian overarticulated incredulously.

"All part of opening out the play that those meddling fools love so much," Abby said. "But don't worry—they've abandoned the idea of the waterfall. Now they're talking about a hot-air balloon."

"I feel ill," Kelly said.

"They'll probably talk themselves out of that as well," Abby said reassuringly, and then changed the subject. "The man who talks in iambs—is he there?"

Holland smiled and matched her rhythm. "For ever and a day, ye wist, fair maid."

The telephone laughed. "Thanks for that 'fair maid.' How are you doing, Holland?"

"Better than ever, thanks."

"Abby," Kelly interrupted, "is it all right with you if I ask Ian to go to a wedding with me?"

"Sure," Abby said amiably. "Ask away. Who's getting married?"

"Ivan Malecki."

"I don't know the name."

Marian said, "My former partner."

"Ah. Well, everyone have a good time!"

Ian took the phone out of the room for a few minutes' private talk with Abby. Marian turned to Holland. "That reminds me—"

"Yes, I'll go to the wedding with you."

Kelly laughed. "Let her ask you first."

"Sorry." He wasn't.

When Ian came back in, he was looking thunderclouds at Kelly. "A wedding? I don't want to go to any wedding."

"Oh, come on, Ian. It'll be fun."

"Why isn't Roger going with you?"

"Roger's a jerk."

"Who's Roger?" Marian asked.

Ian said, "You didn't think he was a jerk the last time you let him come backstage."

"That was two days ago," Kelly retorted. "I know him better now."

"Who's Roger?"

"His feelings will be hurt if you don't ask him," Ian said.

"How can they be? He doesn't even know there *is* a wedding."

Marian rapped a spoon against the side of her glass. "*Who's Roger?*"

"Roger," Ian explained elaborately, "is the love of Kelly's life—and in her heart of hearts, she knows this is so. Why is she doing this cruel thing to Roger?"

Kelly said to Marian, "He's someone I've gone out with a few times, that's all. Roger is not the love of anybody's life, except Roger's." Back to Ian. "Don't be stubborn. You'll get a kick out of this wedding, I promise you."

"Oh? Why is that?"

"Guess who's going to be best man." She looked over to where Marian and Holland were sitting.

Ian looked too. "Holland?"

"Nope," Kelly said gleefully.

The look on Ian Cavanaugh's face told Marian more than anything else yet what a nonsensical situation she'd allowed herself to be dragged into. She groaned and buried her head in her arms on the table. She felt Holland's hand on her back and heard him laugh.

When she raised her head, Ian was laughing too, with his whole body. "Just tell me when and where," he said. "I'll be there!"

* 30 *

Marian went into the stationhouse Monday morning determined not to wait around until Hook Nose had been found.

Perlmutter and O'Toole had already done standard background checks on David Unger and Elmore Zook, finding nothing they didn't expect to find; but now Marian told them to dig deeper. "Forget the paper chase—talk to their acquaintances, the merchants they do business with, like that." She gave them Dowd to help, and told Walker she wanted him to follow Dave Unger if he went anywhere during the day.

"Why Unger and not Zook?" he wanted to know. "My money's on the lawyer."

"Zook will spend the day doing lawyer things," she said. "But O.K. Toys is swarming with IRS accountants, so Unger most likely will avoid the place. See what he does with his time now that things are crashing down around him. And Walker—it's okay if he spots you."

The detective grinned. "Gotcha."

"You other three—before you get going on the background checks, I want you to bring Austin Knowles in for questioning. I'll do the questioning, but you do the bringing. Go get him now, before he leaves home for the day."

Perlmutter groaned. "Lieutenant, Police Regulation Three-Six-Four-A expressly forbids the display of excess energy on Monday mornings."

"Go, go."

They went. Marian called the DA's office and told them what she had in mind, asking if she could dangle a deal in front of Austin Knowles in exchange for information about O.K. Toys. After some consultation, one of the lawyers called back and said go ahead, but don't specify terms. That was good enough for Marian.

When Knowles was brought in, Marian let him sit in an interrogation room for an hour with only a mute police officer for company. When she walked into the room, the architect practically screamed at her for keeping him there incommunicado.

Good.

"Now, Mr. Knowles," she said briskly, "I know that you know what your father was doing at O.K. Toys. That business was just a front. By the way, did he ever make toys?"

"Of course he did!" The man was nervous and hostile. "He was a toymaker—that's what he did. Right up to a few years ago, when he went into distribution only."

"But the company wasn't doing any distributing of toys. Not anymore. It was only pretending to. Somewhere along the line your father got out of the toy business and into . . . what?"

"I don't know! I didn't know the business was a sham until Dave Unger told me the IRS was after him." He ran a hand through his thinning hair. "I thought they were still distributing toys."

"Mr. Knowles, we just don't believe you were unaware of what was going on. Let's cut the crap, shall we? *What kind of racket was your father running?*"

It went on like that for another twenty minutes, with Austin Knowles getting increasingly jumpy until he started yelling at her. At that point, Marian switched her attack.

"Did Dave Unger also tell you that he's the one who ordered the hit on your father?" she asked sharply.

He turned white. "What . . . did you say?"

"He killed your father, Austin. This man you're protecting. He took out the contract on your father."

"I . . . I don't believe it. You just suspect him, you don't really know."

"Oh, we know. It's just a matter of time before we charge him with murder. And that's where you come in. You can save us time. Tell me as much as you know about O.K. Toys."

He continued his denials, growing more agitated by the minute. The man's perpetual edginess could stem from the unsettling loss of both parents followed by the police's pointed interest in him as a suspect. Austin Knowles's naked despair and fear could be that of any man under such pressure. But Marian could not allow herself to doubt his involvement—not now, not during the interrogation. One sign of wavering on her part and she'd lose the advantage she'd built up.

Finally the time came to dangle her bait. "The DA's office is willing to make a deal," she told Knowles. "What kind of deal, I don't know. Reduced sentence, total immunity—it would depend on your degree of involvement with the business."

"I wasn't involved at all!" Then something sank in. "Total immunity?"

"I can't make the deal for the DA. But if the only crime you've committed is withholding evidence, they'll drop that charge, I'm sure. It all depends on what you tell us."

He swallowed visibly. "I want my lawyer."

"Certainly. But a word of advice." Marian leaned toward him across the table. "Get a new lawyer. The one you have now is involved in this mess up to the top of his shiny bald head. Or do you think Elmore Zook wouldn't throw you to the wolves to save his own hide? You know him better than I do. What do you think?"

He swallowed again, trying to lubricate the dry mouth that fear induced. "I've known Elmore Zook for most of my life."

"And he's always been like a father to you—right? You'd trust him the way you'd trust your real father—right?"

Wrong, his eyes said. "Am I under arrest?"

"No. But get yourself a good lawyer, Austin. And do it fast."

"I need a phone."

"Use the one in your office."

He hesitated. "Does that mean I can go?"

"Yes."

He got up slowly, watching her to see if she was toying with him. He shot a glance at the uniformed officer standing silently by the door and darted out.

The bluesuit grinned. "That's one scared rabbit you got there, Lieutenant."

She nodded. "It didn't look like acting to you?"

"Shi—er, heck, no. That guy was ready to piss his—er—"

"Shit, no, that guy was ready to piss his pants," Marian finished for him. "I think so too."

Marian had no problem with using a suspect's guilty fear against him. It was the reason she'd sent Walker to tail Dave Unger. Of the four detectives crowded into her office earlier that morning, she'd picked the one black one. White men got nervous when they saw black men following them.

Sergeant Buchanan waved her over on her way back to

her office. "Gloria Sanchez just called. Robin Muller's boyfriend has skipped town."

"Sensible of him. Do you think he told us everything he knew?"

"Yeah, he did. Once he decided to talk, he couldn't wait to get it all out. I seen it before."

So had Marian. Perlmutter, O'Toole, and Dowd were still out trying to find something more about Dave Unger and Elmore Zook. Walker hadn't called in yet. Noon already; where had the morning gone?

The desk sergeant called to say that Kelly Ingram was downstairs.

When Marian had gotten home from spending Sunday with Holland, she'd found a message from Kelly on her answering machine. Monday was the one day of the week Kelly had free; and on Sundays she had only matinee performances so it was possible for her to get to bed at a decent hour. Kelly's message said she had some errands to run in the morning but they wouldn't take very long and she'd stop by the stationhouse when she was through so they could go have lunch if that was all right with Marian and she wasn't too involved to break away. That was the way she'd said it; all in one breath.

They ate at an Armenian restaurant that Kelly liked and were interrupted by autograph-seekers only four times. "Can you take time to run home with me a minute?" Kelly asked as they were finishing. "I have something there I want you to take a look at."

"Sure. What is it?"

"It's the wedding present I got for Ivan and . . . Claire? I've never met her. Anyway, I want to know if you think it's something they'll use. It's a set of Venetian glassware—goblets, champagne flutes, like that."

Marian's own wedding present was embarrassingly mundane: a TV with a built-in VCR. But Ivan and Claire both had made a point of telling her that's what they wanted. They had a big-screen set for their living room, but they wanted a smaller set with a VCR for the bedroom. For those times they'd feel like taking a break from honeymooning, Marian supposed.

They went back to Kelly's apartment. As Kelly was unlocking the door, Marian said, "I have to use your bathroom. Like immediately."

"Help yourself. I'll go get the present."

Marian turned left down a short hallway to the bathroom while Kelly went on to the living area. Marian took her time in the attractive black-and-white bathroom, using the opportunity to wash with something other than the sickly green liquid soap found in all police stations everywhere. When she left the bathroom, she heard voices. Curious, she walked back down the carpeted hallway.

In the living room, Carla Banner was pointing a gun at Kelly Ingram.

* 31 *

Marian jerked back; Carla hadn't seen her.

Quietly Marian put her coat and bag down on the hall floor and slipped out of her suit jacket. She took a pair of handcuffs from her bag and tucked them into the waistband of her trousers in the back. Then she took her gun out of its holster.

She moved quietly to the end of the short hallway and turned right into the kitchen and from there slipped into the small dining room. She stood flattened against the wall by the open doorway to the living room. Cautiously she looked around the side of the doorway.

Carla was standing with her back to her. The gun in her hand was wobbly; Kelly was staring at it with eyes like saucers. "What do I have to do to make you understand?" Carla's voice was a screech. "I offer to live my life for you, and you . . . and you, you just brush me off as if I were a mosquito! Don't you see? I *love* you, Kelly!"

Kelly managed to speak. "Is that why you're pointing a gun at me?"

"The gun is to make you listen! You don't *listen*, Kelly! I can make your life so much easier for you. You need me. And all I ask in return is to be close to you . . . to help you, to take care of you. You don't have to love me back."

Marian eased through the doorway behind Carla, her gun pointed toward the floor. Kelly, the professional actor, didn't reveal by so much as a flicker of the eye that she'd seen her. She started talking, keeping Carla's attention focused on her. "What kind of life would that be, Carla? Complete self-denial! Nobody should live that way."

"I don't mind, I—"

"You don't have to be a slave. And I don't want a slave. There's got to be something better for you than that. If you—"

Marian stepped up behind Carla and stuck the muzzle of her gun into the younger woman's ear. "Drop the gun, Carla."

Carla shrieked and dropped the gun. "Don't shoot me! Don't shoot me!"

"Hands behind your back." One-handed, still holding her weapon on Carla, Marian put the cuffs on her. She shot a look at Kelly. "You all right?"

"Uh, um, er, yes, I'm all right." Shaken, but okay.

Carla burst out crying. "I wasn't going to hurt her!"

"Yeah, sure." Marian pushed her into a chair and went to the phone to call for a patrol car.

"Marian," Kelly said, perplexed, "it's a prop gun." She was holding the weapon Carla had dropped to the floor. "This part where you're supposed to put the bullets in? It's solid. The holes are just painted on. And the trigger won't pull."

"Let me see."

Kelly handed her the gun. "It's just a stage prop."

And so it was. Kelly had never really been in danger. Carla was howling, tears streaming down her face.

Marian went over to her chair and said in exasperation, "Carla, you not only have the right to remain silent, but I earnestly hope you will do so. *Shut up!*" Carla choked back her howls and gulped and sniffled while Marian read her the rest of her rights.

Only a few minutes later two patrolmen were at the door. Marian handed Carla and the prop gun over to them and said she'd file the arrest report as soon as she got back to Midtown South.

When they were gone, Kelly said, "Poor Carla. She's kind of pathetic, isn't she?"

"Yep," Marian agreed. "She's pathetic, all right. Are you sure you're okay?"

"Hey, I'm fine."

"Maybe you shouldn't be alone. Do you—"

"Oh, *Mar*-ian!" Kelly wailed. "Don't treat me like some fragile flower!"

Marian laughed. "You're right. Sorry. Now, let's figure out how she got in here. Who has a key to this place?"

"Well, you do. And the building super—for deliveries, repairs and stuff."

"Anyone else?"

"No."

"All right, I'll have a word with the super on the way out. And Kelly—stop being so nice to your fans."

Her friend nodded vigorously. "Wicked Witch of the West from now on, that's me."

The super lived in a basement apartment. When Marian asked him why he'd unlocked Kelly Ingram's apartment for a young woman he didn't know, he'd said she'd shown up with a note from Kelly saying to let her in. "I know Ms Ingram's signature," he insisted.

"Signatures can be traced." She told him what had just happened upstairs. He was so upset that Marian almost felt sorry for the man until she learned he was more worried about losing his job than he was about Kelly's safety.

The two patrol officers who'd brought Carla Banner in hadn't kept the arrest a secret. When the desk sergeant saw Marian walk in, he shook his head in mock sadness. "Copaholics, they're the worst. Can't even go to lunch without making an arrest."

Upstairs, Captain Murtaugh gave her a tongue-in-cheek reprimand for approaching such a dangerous criminal without calling for back-up. When she walked through the squadroom, the detectives there stood up and politely applauded; a couple of them said, "Oh, good shew! Good shew!" On her desk was a sheet of paper pretending to be a flyer for the Larch Protective Services—"Guarding Celebrities Our Specialty." She recognized Sergeant Buchanan's handwriting.

Marian finished off the paperwork for Carla's arrest quickly, glad to be done with the incident. Only then did it come to her that she'd not seen the Venetian glassware Kelly had bought as a wedding present.

About an hour later, Walker called. He'd lost Dave Unger. "I'm sorry, Lieutenant. He tried to lose me twice in the midtown crowds, but I kept up with him. Then he ducked into a cab. When I tried to follow in another cab, we got held up by a red light and he got away."

"What did he do today?"

"He went to see Elmore Zook. Spent most of the morning there. Then he had some bank business to tend to. That's where he spotted me, in the bank—and it was hide-and-seek from there on. You want me to stake out his apartment?"

"No, come back in. He knew you were following him, and he ran. That's really what I wanted to know—what he'd do."

"Sorry I lost him," Walker said again.

"Don't worry about it—mission sufficiently accomplished. Come on in."

Walker wasn't the only one to return early. Perlmutter, O'Toole, and Dowd showed up outside her office, looking disgusted. She waved them in. "What?"

Perlmutter said, "We're just wasting our time, Lieutenant. We're not going to find anything on Zook or Unger."

"Convince me," she said.

They gave her names, people they'd spoken to—neighbors, business associates, tradespeople. Zook and Unger both created exactly the same impression on everyone they met: courteous, pleasant, but not outgoing. Neither welcomed quick friendships, even while remaining on amicable terms with almost everyone they encountered. Marian knew from Zook's outburst last Friday that that courteousness was just a façade. Doesn't matter, the three detectives insisted. It was a façade that was well in place; it was one that worked.

"They've just been too damned careful for too many years," Dowd said. "They've left no loose ends for us to pick up. We're just knocking our heads against a wall here."

Perlmutter agreed. "We can go on talking to people until we're blue in the face and we won't know one thing more than we know right now."

O'Toole chimed in, "It's a dead end, Lieutenant."

Marian was convinced; she called off the background check. "We may have another way to get at them." She filled them in on her interrogation of Austin Knowles, stressing his reaction to her mention of a deal and her suggestion that he find a new lawyer.

Perlmutter grinned. "Divide and conquer?"

She nodded. "So now it's Austin Knowles's move. For the time being, we'll play a waiting game." She gave them a big smile. "And that means you can go back to working on those other cases you've been neglecting in order to work on this one!"

They all groaned dramatically and said things like *Goody-goody-gumdrops*. Marian chased them out and got back to work.

Shortly before her shift was due to end, she needed to look for something in the records department. The file cabinets were set up in rows with narrow aisles between them; never enough space. Marian found the drawer she was looking for and pulled it open.

While she was reading a file, she heard a couple of people come in and open a file drawer the next aisle over. She couldn't see them, but she recognized the voices of Sergeant Buchanan and one of the detectives on his squad. She paid no attention to what they were saying and went on reading her file.

Until something Buchanan said jerked her back to attention. "I never thought I'd end my days takin' orders from some dumb cunt," he groused. "When Murtaugh told me he was bringin' in a fuckin' broad as the new lieutenant, I almost asked him how good a lay she was."

The other detective guffawed. "You think he's really poking her?"

Buchanan snorted. "You gotta ask? How else did she get him to recommend her for the job? But if I was gonna have a piece on the side, she'd look a helluva lot better'n Larch!"

They both laughed at that. "Knockers ain't bad," the detective said. "But fuck, they have to be dogs to wanna be cops," the detective said.

"Yeah," Buchanan agreed, "but Larch, she thinks she's Supercop. She hasn't put her foot in it yet, but give her time. These pushy bitches always end up screwin' themselves."

Marian quietly closed the drawer and moved to the end of the row of file cabinets where they could see her. "Buchanan." Both men jumped. "My office. Now." She walked away.

When he followed her into her office, his face was a mixture of uneasiness and defiance. "Look, Lieutenant—"

"What the *hell* do you think you're doing, talking about me like that?" she snapped. "And spreading that story that I slept my way into this job—you're maligning two superior officers, Captain Murtaugh as well as me."

"Lieutenant, it dint mean nothin'. It's just the way guys talk when they get together."

"Well, the 'guys' are going to have to clean up their act. We have police regulations, Buchanan, and you *will* obey them. Such talk will not be tolerated—ever. You have a woman detective on your squad, and there's another on Campos's squad. Do you talk about them that way behind their backs? Or do you say it to their faces? What can they do about it? You're the *sergeant*, Buchanan. You set the standard your detectives follow. You just now taught that detective in there that it's okay to call me a cunt and to spread a rumor that I whored my way into my position."

"Hey, you got it all wrong. We was just kiddin'. He knew I was kiddin'. Can'tcha take a joke?"

"Don't you *dare* pull that bullshit on me!" Marian flared. "All right, Buchanan, this is a warning. It's going on your record. If it happens again, I'll have you up for disciplinary action."

"Now, wait a minute—"

"No, you wait a minute. I *will* discipline you if I have to. Or if you want to transfer out of Midtown South, I'll sign the papers right now."

His face turned red with anger. "I been workin' this precinct for fourteen years—"

"Then don't blow it now. I understand that men of your generation have trouble with women in authority. But do you know something? *I don't care.* Adjust—or get left behind.

And if I hear one more sexist remark out of that filthy mouth of yours, I'm going to throw the book at you. Do you understand?"

He looked as if he wanted to hit her. "Yeah. Oh yeah. I understand."

She stared at that lived-in face and wondered if she'd gotten through to him at all. "For your own sake, Buchanan, I hope you do. I mean that. Now get out of here. You make me sick."

He left without another word.

Marian sat down at her desk, resting her head on one hand and feeling lower than she'd felt in a long time. *We was just kiddin' . . . Can'tcha take a joke?* Did he really think he could smooth over the whole thing, that she'd let him get away with calling her a cunt? Did the men who thought like that expect her to *win them over* by going along, by trying to make them *like* her?

To hell with that.

And here she'd thought Buchanan was one of the friendlies. She picked up the paper he'd left on her desk, the one advertising Larch Protective Services—part of the general razzing she'd taken after her arrest of Dangerous Carla Banner. She balled up the paper and tossed it at the wastebasket. What a hypocrite the man was.

On her way out, an utterly silly thought popped into her head: *No wonder he never asked me to call him Buck.*

* 32 *

On Tuesday, they caught Hook Nose.

A sharp-eyed bluesuit riding in a patrol car spotted him coming out of Tiffany's around one o'clock. The officer and his partner nailed him just as he was stopping a cab. A quick frisk revealed no weapon, but he was carrying a Tiffany box containing a pair of diamond earrings. Somewhere a woman was waiting for this murderous man.

His name was Thomas Schumacher, or at least that's what his ID said he was calling himself, and he was carrying a room key from the Regency. A hastily arranged search warrant for his hotel suite turned up nothing of interest. But the warrant also covered the hotel safe and there the detectives hit pay dirt: banded stacks of thousand-dollar bills and, more important, the murder weapon—locked in a velvet-lined carrying case.

They had him cold.

Schumacher understood that, and steadfastly refused any comment until he'd talked to his lawyer. When the lawyer got there, a lantern-jawed man named Jasper, a long consultation between attorney and client ended with Jasper's indicating they were willing to talk about a deal. But Lieutenant Marian Larch took a chance and put Schumacher in a line-up, summoning the witnesses who'd been on the subway when Robin Muller was shot. All three placed Schumacher on the seat next to Muller at the time she died.

Now the police were in a position of even greater bargaining strength. Captain Murtaugh issued an order that no mention of Schumacher's capture was to be made, even impressing upon the arresting officers the importance of not telling anyone—not their wives, not their fellow cops, not anyone—of the big catch they'd made that day. He went out of his way to make sure Jasper would cooperate; the lawyer had nothing to gain by defying the captain's wishes. The police had an advantage over Virgil now, and Murtaugh made sure they all understood that losing that advantage through careless talk would be a career-ending mistake.

Their shift had ended for the day, but no one working on the case had left. Another lawyer appeared: Assistant District Attorney Julia Perry, whom Marian knew only by reputation. The bargaining was short; Perry made it clear at the outset that there would be no deal without full disclosure on Schumacher's part. Jasper first asked for full immunity for his client in exchange for his information. Perry said forget it, while the cops just laughed. Jasper had evidently advised his client already that that one wouldn't go, so the bargaining over a reduced sentence began. Perry and Jasper quickly reached agreement, with Perry stressing that the information must lead to the capture of Virgil or the deal was off. Schumacher agreed to the terms and was ready to make his statement.

The interrogation room had the close smell and feel of any small space with too many people packed into it. Schumacher, his lawyer, the Assistant DA, Marian, Captain Murtaugh, and Gloria Sanchez from the Ninth Precinct were there; Captain DiFalco was out of town. On the other side of the one-way mirror, Sergeant Buchanan and the four other detectives who'd worked the case were watching. Gloria's partner, Detective Roberts, was observing as well. Marian started the tape recorder, gave the date and the names of those present.

"Who is Virgil?" she asked.

"I don't know," Schumacher said.

Gloria Sanchez threw up her arms.

"This," Marian said heavily, "is not a good start."

"I never met Virgil," Schumacher replied sharply. "I speak to him on the phone, but I've never seen him."

Start at the beginning.

Thomas Schumacher was a sort of circuit contract killer. He'd work one city until his MO became noticeable and then move on. Periodically he'd change his MO and then work the circuit again. A lot of his earlier hits in New York had been made to look like accidents; he'd been paid extra for those. He had contacts in a dozen cities, and this time he'd come to New York from St. Louis.

Perry demanded the names of these other contacts. Jasper reminded her the deal was for Virgil only and his client was under no obligation to incriminate himself further. Captain Murtaugh pointed out that the NYPD's only interest was in putting Virgil out of business, but the Assistant DA was adamant; she'd seen a way to make a big case even bigger and she wasn't about to let go. Schumacher put an end to it by agreeing to provide the names of his contacts.

Everyone in the room stared at him. Jasper tried to caution his client but Schumacher shrugged him off. "But why?" the lawyer asked.

"I'm running out of time," Schumacher answered cryptically.

Julia Perry was in seventh heaven; the killer had just handed her the case of her life. Schumacher recited a list of names—which were probably phony—and phone numbers, which were undoubtedly real.

Marian had watched all the bargaining with contempt, contempt for the procedure and even more contempt for the man Schumacher. "How did you first find Virgil?" she asked.

Virgil had found him, Schumacher said. Through a mutual contact in Chicago. All arrangements were made over the phone.

How did it work?

Virgil paid only when the contract had been fulfilled, Schumacher told them. He was to wait by his phone in his suite at the Regency at noon every day. If there was no call by twelve-fifteen, that meant Virgil had no work for him that day. Virgil had also made it clear that if ever Schumacher was not there to receive the phone call, he'd be off the payroll for good.

Gloria Sanchez said, "So that's why you're running out of time." Suddenly a lot of things fell into place. Schumacher's only bargaining chip was his link to Virgil; if he missed the phone call that could come as soon as the next day, that link would be severed and Schumacher would be left with nothing. So he needed the quick bargaining, the quick statement. If the police were to catch Virgil, Schumacher would have to be sitting by his phone every day at noon until he called.

"So what does Virgil say in these phone calls?" Murtaugh asked.

Virgil would name a time and place and hang up. The time was always that same day, and the place always a public one. A courier would meet Schumacher with an envelope containing one or two photographs plus a data sheet identifying the target. Once the contract was fulfilled, another phone call would name another time and place where a different courier would bring him his money.

"Wait a minute," Gloria Sanchez said. "You never saw the same courier twice?"

Frequently, Schumacher said. But the courier who brought π the information envelope was never the one who delivered the money. Virgil had two groups of couriers. The first was mostly women just trying to earn a buck who clearly had no idea of what Virgil's organization was. But the second group had to be different, Schumacher reasoned; they were entrusted with carrying large sums of money. Schumacher's theory was that the first group was undergoing a tryout unknown to themselves; Virgil probably hired people he judged to have a potential for corruption, who could be developed for more important positions in his organization.

Marian asked if Robin Muller had ever delivered an information envelope to him.

A flicker of surprise showed in Schumacher's hard eyes. No. He'd not known Muller was one of Virgil's people.

And that was it. That was what Schumacher had to offer.

The killer had had personal contact only with the outermost fringe of Virgil's organization, the couriers. But the couriers were the link to the man Robin Muller had called the paymaster. The police's next step was obvious.

Schumacher was returned to his cell; both lawyers departed. The detectives who'd observed the interrogation went home, leaving Marian, Captain Murtaugh, and Gloria Sanchez to work out the details. They decided to return the killer to his suite at the Regency the next morning; they'd keep him there under guard until Virgil called, thus avoiding the risks present in moving him back and forth from a jail cell every day. Detectives from both the Ninth Precinct and Midtown South would stay with Schumacher for every second. Murtaugh insisted on four-man shifts; the killer was just too dangerous to go with any fewer. Marian and Gloria drew up a schedule.

"An organization as efficiently run as Virgil's," Marian remarked, "has got to keep records. Lots and lots of nice incriminating records."

"Yeah," Gloria said happily. "We're gonna close a lot of homicide cases once we get those records."

"And maybe even more. I'm thinking of O.K. Toys. Maybe Virgil's records will tell us what kind of dirty business Oliver Knowles's company was up to."

Murtaugh raised a quizzical eyebrow. "What makes you think Virgil is interested in the reasons people hire him?"

Marian shrugged. "It's a tremendous potential for blackmail, Captain. Virgil's in a great position to extract money from people. You think he's not going to use it?"

The captain conceded the probability. "But you can't count on it. Dave Unger's the only way you're going to find out what the toy company was being used for. And he's not talking."

Gloria said, "But when Unger's name shows up in Virgil's records, we won't have to prove motive. Just the fact that he hired Virgil will be enough."

"It's not right," Marian grumbled. "We have to depend on a master criminal to solve a lesser crime for us? It shouldn't work that way."

Murtaugh smiled. "Offends your sense of propriety, does it, Larch?"

"It's not right," Marian repeated.

* 33 *

"You're in trouble," the voice on the phone said.

Midmorning of the day following the capture of Thomas Schumacher, Elmore Zook had called Marian to issue a few legalistic-sounding threats. He blamed her for losing a client; it seemed Austin Knowles had followed Marian's advice and hired a different lawyer. That news heartened Marian so much that she barely heard Zook's threats. Another possible breakthrough?

"I don't think you understand what you've done," Zook said icily. "I've represented the Knowles family ever since about two months after I received my law degree. And now I've lost Austin because some lady cop doesn't know what else to do and so plays at divide and conquer. You simply can't use your badge to meddle in private business."

"Mr. Zook, I can give advice to anyone I please," Marian said. "But I can't compel anyone to follow that advice. And don't threaten me. You're wasting your own time as well as mine."

"We'll see whether it's a waste of time or not. I'm going to hit you with a civil suit unless Austin comes back. He listened to you once, he might listen again. You talk to Austin."

"A civil suit?" she asked with interest. "Charging me with what?"

"Violation of police authority," Zook said coolly. "You talk to Austin." He hung up.

That was exactly what she was going to do: talk to Austin. She called his office; the architect's secretary said he was at the Wall Street construction site. Marian grabbed her coat and bag. Dowd wasn't at his desk; he and Walker were on this morning's guard duty at the Regency with two detectives from the Ninth. Sergeant Buchanan had been keeping out of her way—probably just as well. She told Perlmutter where she was going. He offered to come with her; she said get back to work. He grinned and shrugged; it was worth a try.

Marian took the subway, the quickest way of getting downtown. When she found the construction site, she saw it was mostly idle. A few men were at work putting up some temporary hurricane fencing. But none of the huge earth-moving machines Marian expected to see were on view; the ground must be too hard to work this time of year. Austin Knowles was in the foreman's shack going over blueprints.

When he saw Marian at the door, he asked the foreman to leave them alone for a few minutes. The other man left with a questioning glance at Marian. She perched on a tall stool and examined the man she'd come to see.

For the first time since she'd met him, Austin Knowles was not a bundle of nerves. He appeared resigned, depressed—but no longer jumpy. *He's decided to talk*, Marian thought with a surge of adrenaline. "Elmore Zook just called me," she said.

Austin gave her a lopsided grin. "He's not too pleased with me."

Nor with me. "You've got a new lawyer."

"Yes. And he's persuaded me to tell the police what I know about my father's business dealings. I can't tell you much, because I don't know much. But my attorney says it will be enough for you to know what to do."

"That's what you should have done right at the start. When do we get to hear your statement?"

"My attorney's negotiating with the DA's office. We'll be in as soon as he's able to work out some sort of deal for me. I'm under orders not to talk to you at all unless he's present. So I'm afraid I'll have to ask you to leave."

"Who is your new attorney?"

"James Archer. Archer, Carlisle, and Wickes."

"That's a big firm. Archer—the head honcho's doing the negotiating? Not one of his associates?"

"He says he wants to handle it himself."

Another lawyer sniffing out a big case, Marian thought with distaste.

Austin Knowles misinterpreted the look on her face. "We *are* coming in, Lieutenant." He looked sadly at the blueprints spread out on the worktable. "I just wanted to make sure that this last job is done right. Now, I can't talk to you anymore."

Marian didn't argue; she knew a defeated man when she saw one. She left him alone.

It was getting on toward noon. Marian looked for an eatery that had a pay telephone and found a fairly clean lunch counter called Rusty's. She asked for a cup of coffee and sat waiting for her beeper to sound. But twelve-fifteen came and went with no signal from the device; Virgil had not called today. Marian ordered lunch.

When she'd finished, she thought that as long as she was out, she might as well drop in on Dave Unger. The air was brisk and cold, and something vaguely resembling sunlight was shining in the streets. Marian stopped a cab and gave the driver Unger's address.

She had nothing new to say to Unger, and Murtaugh would give her hell if he knew she was going to see a murder

BARBARA PAUL

suspect alone. But Marian had never gotten a sense of personal menace from the man; he was a long-distance killer, hiring someone else to do his dirty work for him. The background check had turned up the information that Unger was a CPA who'd started in Billing at O.K. Toys and worked his way up to manager. Just another all-American success story. Nevertheless, Marian unfastened the flap on her shoulder holster. Maybe she should have brought Perlmutter after all.

Unger was at home alone, although the spacious apartment showed indications that both a woman and children were living there. "Zook told me not to talk to you," Unger said.

"I'll talk," Marian replied. "You listen."

He didn't offer her a seat. "I'm listening."

"You know your days are numbered, don't you?" she asked rhetorically. "This thing is coming to a head. It will go much easier for you if you cooperate now, when you still have something to offer. Deals are made every day."

"I can't," he said tightly.

"Sure you can. What are you afraid of? We'll keep our side of the bargain."

He just shook his head.

Marian was exasperated. "I don't understand you! The IRS is going to send you away for a thousand years and we'll add another thousand on top of that with a homicide charge. You can get yourself reduced sentences on both charges just by talking now before it's too late—and you don't say a word!"

Unger spread his hands helplessly. "Lieutenant, I'm an accountant. I'm not a policy-maker."

You had your policy-maker killed, you sonuvabitch. The two stared at each other until Marian gave it up as hopeless and left, thinking the trip hadn't been worth the cab fare.

Back at the station, she dumped her coat and bag in her office and went to see Murtaugh. She told him about Elmore Zook's threatened civil action.

"He's blowing smoke," Murtaugh scoffed. "There's nothing he can sue you for—he's just trying to intimidate you." He squinted at her. "Did he?"

"No. But I thought you ought to know."

"Right." A pause. "How's the Buchanan problem?"

Marian smiled wryly. "He's hiding from me."

When she'd reported the incident in the records department, Murtaugh had exploded; Marian had never seen him so angry. The denigrating sexist talk was bad enough, but innuendo that Murtaugh had engineered Marian's promotion in exchange for sexual favors was what really got to him; the captain was just as jealous of his good name as Marian was of hers. His first impulse had been to have it out with Buchanan, but Marian had asked him not to. Buchanan would undoubtedly take a reprimand from a man more seriously than he'd taken one from her; but he had to learn that he *must* listen to her. Getting the captain to fight her battles for her would just reinforce Buchanan's attitudes toward women in authority.

Murtaugh reluctantly agreed. But he no longer addressed the other man by the friendly *Buck*; now it was the more formal *Sergeant* or just *Buchanan*. The whole station was aware of the ice that had suddenly appeared between the captain and one of his sergeants.

Marian reminded Murtaugh that she was taking some personal time the next day, for Ivan's wedding.

"What if Virgil calls?" he asked. "What if you have to miss the wedding?"

"Then Ivan will kill me," Marian said simply.

* 34 *

Virgil did not call on Thursday.

Almost cheering with relief, Marian was out of the stationhouse by twelve-twenty. Captain Murtaugh, god bless him, had told no one that she was acting as best man in her former partner's wedding, so she was able to escape without the razzing that would otherwise have been her lot.

The wedding rehearsal had gone smoothly the night before. Mrs. Yelincic was in her element, playing both The Great Organizer and The Perfect Hostess rolled into one. Marian met the members of the wedding party she didn't know, including two of the ushers; the other two were police detectives she'd known as long as Ivan had. All during the rehearsal, the matron of honor—Claire's older sister, Angela—had kept staring at Marian as if she were some sort of freak. A little of that went a long way; Marian quickly decided she didn't care for Angela.

Right before they broke up for the evening, Claire had whispered to Marian that Ivan had asked her to be his best man because she was the only one of his friends he could trust to make things work. That's when Marian started getting nervous.

Shower and shampoo, and then Marian took out the dress she'd bought for the wedding. She hadn't bought a dress in about two years, and she knew she'd never wear this one again. Not her sort of thing at all. Too see-what-a-pretty-doll-I-am for her tastes, right down to the touch of delicate lace at the neckline. Kelly had talked her into buying it. Marian had asked her friend to help her find the right sort of thing, as there didn't seem to be much precedent for what female best men should wear. The dress was even a color Marian normally avoided, a rich beige just enough darker than bridal white so that she wouldn't seem to be stealing Claire's thunder. Kelly said the color set off Marian's dark hair just right.

Marian checked for the tenth time to make sure the ring hadn't jumped out of its box. Time to go pick up Ivan.

She'd ordered a limousine for the occasion; Marian didn't want to have to worry about traffic, possible flat tires, and getting lost in Queens on top of all the other things she had on her mind. The driver was a talkative sort who regaled her all the way with stories about rock stars and tennis players he'd picked up at the airport.

Ivan was actually standing out on the sidewalk with his luggage waiting for her when they pulled up. "My god, I thought you'd never get here!" he screamed.

"I'm half an hour early," she replied with a calmness she was far from feeling. "Get in."

"Nervous?" the driver asked. He put Ivan's luggage in the trunk.

Ivan had the envelopes waiting for her, the ones with the checks to pay off various people who expected to collect for their services later in the day. Marian put the envelopes in her new purse.

"Do you have the ring?"

"Yes, Ivan, I have the ring."

"Show me!"

She showed him.

"Okay, okay. Don't lose it! Maybe I'd better take it?"

"I'm not going to lose the ring. Try to relax, Ivan. My god. Take deep breaths."

He concentrated on breathing deeply. The limo moved smoothly through Queens traffic toward St. Stanislaus Church. After a few minutes, Ivan had calmed down somewhat.

"Oops," said the driver.

Ivan sat bolt-upright. "*What do you mean, 'Oops'?*"

"I think I missed a turn back there," the driver said. "Can I get to the church from here?"

"Omigod . . . I don't know! Where are we? Marian, where should he turn?"

Marian pointed out that *he* was the one who lived in Queens, not she.

"Let's try this," the driver said and turned right.

"We're not going to make it!" Ivan said in a high voice. "I'm going to be late to my own wedding!"

"We're not going to be late," Marian said soothingly. "We're early, remember?"

"Plenny a time," the driver agreed. "Hey, here we are! Right back on track. No problem."

"No problem." Ivan sank back in his seat. "I'm never gonna make it. I'm never gonna make it."

"Of course you are," Marian said. "The ceremony will be over before you know it—and then we'll all dance at your wedding. You're going to remember this day for the rest of your life."

She kept talking to him, trying to keep her voice level and reassuring. By the time they reached the church, Ivan wasn't exactly calm but he was no longer jumping out of his skin. He sprang out of the limo and ran into the church.

"Eager, ain't he?" said the driver.

Or scared. "Listen, you'll need to move Ivan's luggage to the bridal limo when it gets here. As soon as—"

"How do I know which one it is?"

"I'm telling you. As soon as the bridal party gets here, look for Mrs. Yelincic. She's easy to spot—she'll be the one giving orders to everyone else. Mrs. Yelincic will have the key to the trunk of the bridal limo."

"Yelincic, check."

"We'll be leading the procession from the church to the reception hall. You're sure you know the way?"

"Yeah, yeah, yeah, I know the way. Don't worry. Just you and me?"

"And one other. If you'll pull the car up enough to leave room for the bridal limo, you can stay right here. I already checked with the priest."

Marian watched him move the limousine forward a few feet; that was all right, then. She went into the church and down the long center aisle. Just before the altar she turned right, toward the little room where Father Kuzak had said they could wait until the ceremony began. Her route took her past the musician hired to play at the wedding; he was just sitting down at the . . . synthesizer, Marian saw, not organ.

"Hiya, Sally," he said vaguely as she passed.

Marian said *Hiya* back. Sally?

Ivan was standing in front of the full-length mirror placed there expressly to reassure nervous bridegrooms, grimacing at his reflection. "How do I look?"

He looked great. "You look great, Ivan."

Something in her tone convinced him. "Yeah?" He grinned, at last beginning to realize he was supposed to be enjoying himself. "Great, huh?"

"No question." Marian slipped out of her coat and Ivan

saw her dress for the first time. "Hey, so do you! That's a terrific dress! It makes you look . . . soft and feminine."

She glared at him.

Father Kuzak came bustling in, looking for all the world like a bald Peter Lorre. "Are we all ready, then? A good day for a wedding, a good day! Do you need anything? May I get you something?"

"Thanks, Father," Ivan said, "I think we're all set."

"Good, good. There's orange juice in that little refrigerator and you know where the restroom is. I have something to attend to, but I'll be back to get you in good time." He bustled back out.

The synthesizer music started. "The first guests must be arriving," Marian said. "I'd better go check on the ushers. I'll be right—"

"What the hell is he playing?" Ivan interrupted.

"What?"

"God, that's awful stuff! Why's he playing that?"

Marian, who was tone deaf, ventured no opinion. "He's not playing the music you and Claire selected?"

"No! I don't want *that* played at our wedding! That's awful!" A note of panic was creeping into his voice.

"Ivan, I'll take care of it. Keep calm. See, I'm going to take care of it. I'm going now. Deep breaths. Deep breaths."

He was gulping in air when she left the room and slipped up to where the musician was sitting. She put her mouth next to his ear and said, "You're playing the wrong music."

"Hanh?"

"It's the wrong music."

"No, it isn't."

"The bridegroom says it is. Stop."

He brought what he was playing to a close and started shuffling through some sheet music. He pulled out a typewritten list of the numbers he was to play. "See, that was right! The Hamilton/Burger wedding."

Marian ground her teeth. "This is the Yelincic/Malecki wedding."

His eyes grew large. "No shit." He coughed a laugh. "Wow. Imagine that." He shuffled through the papers some more until he came up with a list headed *Yelincic/Malecki.* "That one?"

"That one."

He began to play. The few early guests had watched the interchange curiously.

In the little waiting room, Ivan was looking relieved. "That's the right music."

"I'm going to check on the ushers. I'll be right back."

She didn't want to walk back down the center aisle with guests already seated, so she had to go through the church building to the back door and then around to the front. Her new shoes were starting to pinch.

Three ushers were waiting there, smiling and joking with one another. Missing was a young relative of Ivan's whom everyone called Bingo. "Where's Bingo?" she asked. The other three hadn't seen him.

Marian fished an address book out of her new purse. She found a phone in the vestry and called Bingo's number. No answer.

Out front again, the guests were beginning to arrive in a steady trickle. Ivan's father was dead, but his mom arrived with two of his aunts. Marian had run out without a coat, looking up and down the street for Bingo. She began to feel chilled and stepped inside the church entrance. "I like that dress," one of the ushers told her. "Very feminine, very soft." She managed not to snarl at him.

A cab pulled up, and much to Marian's relief, it was

Bingo who climbed out. But when the cab drove away, Bingo stayed standing in the street, swaying in time to some privately heard music.

Marian hurried out to him. "Come on, Bingo—you're late!"

He gave her a big goofy grin. "Issh ne'er too late."

She stared at him, horrified. "You're sloshed!"

"To the gills," he agreed amiably.

She steered him out of the street and then went to get one of the police detectives serving as an usher. "Bingo's drunk," she said, "and you've got to sober him up. I don't care how you do it, but do it. You have twenty minutes at most before the bridal party gets here." He grunted and went off to collect Bingo while Marian informed the other ushers they were going to have to do double duty.

A number of guests were lingering on the steps, chatting for a few minutes before going inside. Marian was heading around to the back door of the church again when a white stretch limo pulled up. The waiting guests gasped when Ian Cavanaugh stepped out, and a titter of excitement ran through the small crowd when he reached in to help Kelly Ingram alight. The third person to emerge was Holland, looking as if he could think of one or two places he'd rather be at the moment.

"That dark-eyed broody one," Marian heard one guest say to another, "that's Kelly Ingram's bodyguard. He used to be with the FBI!"

Marian rolled her eyes and hurried around to the back of the church. How did these things get started?

Ivan wasn't in the little waiting room.

Beginning to feel just a mite hassled, she started hunting for him. She found him tap-dancing in the vestry.

"It relaxes me," he explained. "I was getting claustrophobic in there!"

She dragged him back to the waiting room. They waited in silence. Marian's feet were seriously hurting.

Before long Father Kuzak popped in to say the bridal party had arrived; they'd be starting momentarily.

Then it was time. Ivan led the way, followed by his best man. They took their place by the altar and turned to face the main church entrance, where Claire would be coming in. A number of guests were openly gaping.

Ivan said out of the side of his mouth, "Hey, they're all staring at *you!*"

"What did you expect?" she muttered back.

Then the ushers came to stand behind them—all four of them, she was happy to see. Bingo's hair was sopping wet and plastered down neatly against his head; a cold-water spigot could do wonders in a pinch. Marian gave the rescuing usher a wink.

The musician started to play again. Down the aisle came Angela, the matron of honor. Three bridesmaids followed. Then a tiny flower girl. The musician swung into a new tune that everyone recognized as entrance music even though it was questionable whether any of them had ever heard it before.

And here came the bride. Claire was stunning, and Marian could feel Ivan puffing up with pride. Even shadowy Mr. Yelincic looked proud as he led his daughter down the aisle. Marian began to relax for the first time that day. It was really happening.

Ivan and Claire had written their own vows, but Father Kuzak had not read them at the rehearsal, simply saying *And here I read the words provided by the bride and groom.* He started reading now.

Ivan and Claire exchanged a puzzled look. Father Kuzak droned on, unnoticing. "Do something!" Claire whispered.

"Hsst! Father!" Ivan couldn't make him hear. He cleared his throat and said aloud, "Father!"

The priest looked up, surprised.

"Those aren't the vows we wrote."

"But surely they are!" Father Kuzak whispered.

"No, they're not," Claire whispered back. "Those are not our vows."

Marian stepped closer and looked at the typed pages the priest had inserted into his book. She tapped a fingernail on the name penciled in at the top: *Hamilton/Burger*.

"Oh, my goodness!" The priest was mortified. "How could that have—I've never—"

"Father Kuzak," Marian said, low, "go get the right vows."

"Go . . . yes. I'll go get the right vows." He scurried off.

A murmur ran through the congregation. Marian looked over her shoulder at the wedding guests; they looked puzzled, concerned. All except Holland, who was sitting there with a big laugh on his face. And Kelly and Ian, the professionals, who were maintaining perfect poker faces. She caught sight of Mrs. Yelincic, who looked ready to die.

"I can't *believe* this is happening!" Claire hissed.

"It's just a little delay," Ivan said. "He'll find them." He shot a look at Marian. "Well, you told me this would be a day I'd remember the rest of my life."

"I gotta pee!" the little flower girl announced. Shushing sounds. Father Kuzak came hurrying back with the right vows. "We shall resume," he announced with as much dignity as he could muster.

This time they made it. Ivan and Claire were well and truly wed. The musician gave them a jazzy exit, none of the women tripped on their long gowns, and Bingo managed to escort his bridesmaid-partner down the aisle without falling on his face.

Marian dashed off to the little waiting room and grabbed her coat and purse. The musician was gathering up his sheet music when she handed him his envelope. "Thanks, Sally," he said.

She found Father Kuzak sitting on a hall bench fanning himself with a prayer book. "I don't know how that happened," he said when he saw her coming.

"Don't worry about it," Marian said. "It worked out just fine." She handed him his envelope. Her feet *really* hurt.

He opened the envelope. "Oh, that's very generous, I'm sure—but I was rather expecting more."

"Mrs. Yelincic said you'd say that." She hurried out to the church entrance.

There was no receiving line, for which Marian was grateful. On the church steps, a photographer was trying to get everyone in the wedding party together. Marian heard a snore; she found Bingo asleep on one of the pews. She woke him up and got him out front for the picture.

The photographer kept trying to move Marian over with the bridesmaids until Ivan made him understand she was *supposed* to be standing in the best man's spot. The picture was finally taken.

Marian gave Claire a hug and whispered, "I think Ivan is one lucky man." Claire was glowing.

The crowd outside the church started breaking up, going to their cars for the procession to the reception hall. A small group of admirers was gathered around Kelly and Ian, who were both laughing and chatting away. Marian saw Holland heading toward her.

He was looking at her dress. Marian's hands formed into fists. *If he tells me how soft and feminine I'm looking, I may hit him.*

"Well, well," Holland said with a smile. "I see you can

dress just as conventionally as everyone else when you put your mind to it."

She kissed him.

"That's nice," said Mrs. Yelincic, passing by.

"Must we to go to the reception?" Holland asked.

Marian said yes. "I have to toast the bride and groom." Kelly and Ian wouldn't be going; they had a performance that evening. Marian slipped into her coat. "We're in the first limo."

One final check to make sure all the wedding party had rides. "Are we ready?" she called out.

"Ready!" a dozen happy voices sang.

Holland was standing by the open door of the limo. As Marian climbed in, the driver said, "Hey, that Mrs. Yelincic is really something, ain't she? She invited me to the reception."

"So glad you hit it off," Marian said, and collapsed.

* 35 *

Marian dragged into her office the next morning both looking and feeling as if she had a hangover. But she'd drunk very little at the wedding reception; it was the day itself that had been the intoxicant.

Captain Murtaugh stuck his head in the door. "How'd it go?"

Marian sighed. "Well, we got through it. And Ivan established a new wedding tradition by dancing with his best man."

Murtaugh grinned. "Did the guests know about you ahead of time?"

"Only a few. There was lots and lots of staring."

"But did you have fun?"

She thought back over the previous day's craziness. "Yeah. I had fun."

He waggled his eyebrows at her. "Told you you would."

When he left, Marian took out a thermos of black coffee she'd had filled on her way in. She was pouring her first cup when Sergeant Campos appeared in the door. Marian swallowed her coffee and looked at him balefully.

Campos said, "I just wanted to know if Walker and Dowd have been working out okay."

"Absolutely. They're doing good work."

The sergeant actually smiled. "I told you they were good detectives."

I never said they weren't. "And you were right."

"Well, uh, that's all I wanted to know." He left.

Perlmutter came in.

Marian gave him the bent eye. "If you came in here to say 'I told you so,' you're going to be walking a beat before the day's over."

"But I didn't tell you so," he said worriedly. "That's what's bothering me." He sat down. "When we were doing background checks, one little thing popped up that I didn't pay any attention to at the time, but now—"

"What is it?"

"Unger's secretary . . . name's Iris—"

"I met her."

"She was afraid O.K. Toys would close and she'd lose her job. Both the police and the IRS poking around—you know. But here's the part that's worrying me. She said, 'Mr. Unger even closed the Zurich account he'd just opened—he wouldn't do that if the business wasn't in trouble, would he?' "

"So? Big-time criminals have numbered Swiss accounts as a matter of course. You mean he's accumulating as much cash as he can? Planning to disappear?"

"No, Lieutenant. She said *the Zurich account he'd just opened.* A new account."

"Huh."

"I don't know what it means."

"Nor do I," Marian murmured. "Okay, Perlmutter, let me think about it. Thanks."

She sat pondering this new detail and drinking her coffee. When she'd worked out a possible explanation, she went to see Murtaugh.

"A new account?" he said with a frown. "Why now?"

"Perhaps because he never needed one before. Because he didn't have anything to put in the account."

"I don't follow."

"Captain, what if the reason we haven't been able to find out what O.K. Toys is doing is that they haven't done it yet?"

He shot her a look. "They've just been setting it up?"

"Could be, don't you think?" She sat down, facing him across his desk. "It would take a lot of time just to build their cover—the falsified financial records, the phony invoices they had printed. If it's a new scam, then Oliver Knowles didn't have anything to do with it. Unger couldn't start until after Knowles retired. Then on one of his infrequent visits to the office, Knowles could have stumbled across something—invoices he knew couldn't be right or whatever. And so Unger had to get rid of him."

"Which leaves Zook out of it?"

"Unger's the only one who could have manipulated the switch from toy distribution to whatever illegal enterprise he had in mind. He's the man in charge. And it has to have been a big operation, to require this much preparation. Big operations require records-keeping. He'd have to set that up as well as the phony books."

"But the IRS has been there all this week. They would have found those real records."

Marian leaned her forearms on his desk. "Captain, those IRS agents are accountants—they're not computer people. There are all sorts of ways to hide files electronically. If Unger used a computer security specialist to set up his system, the IRS wouldn't even know that other stuff was there."

Murtaugh pulled at his lower lip. "Maybe we ought to get our own computer people in there."

"That's what I'm thinking. The dates on the files would be significant. They'd tell us whether the illicit system was set up before or after Oliver Knowles retired."

The captain nodded. "All right, let me find out if the police computer people are equipped to handle a case like this. It sounds pretty specialized to me."

Marian went back to her office feeling uneasy and irritated. That theory she'd just put to Captain Murtaugh could turn out to be a rough approximation of the truth . . . or it could be a fairy tale. She had no substantiation for any of it. It angered her that eleven days after his murder, she still didn't know whether Oliver Knowles was a criminal or an innocent victim.

And then at noon, Virgil called.

The meet was set for three that afternoon at the Guggenheim. By two the Spiral Gallery was filled with NYPD detectives wearing wires and showing an intense interest in the new "Art of the Future" exhibit.

The phone call had not instructed Thomas "Hook Nose" Schumacher to carry or wear anything special to identify himself; that meant the courier he was meeting was known to him. Known by sight only, Schumacher stressed; names were never exchanged. Four of the many cops in the Guggenheim had only one assignment: Make sure Schumacher doesn't bolt.

The plan was not to arrest the courier but to follow her, or him. Robin Muller's procedure had been to deliver her envelope of murder instructions and then go straight to meet the paymaster. It was the paymaster the police were interested in; he was one step closer to Virgil. Detective Walker had argued for picking the paymaster up rather than risk losing him in the crowd. Detective Perlmutter said they'd be blowing a chance to get all the way to Virgil if they picked him up prematurely. Marian decided to continue the tail.

It would be a close tail, with someone sticking next to the paymaster at all times. The detectives doing the following would shift positions constantly, so the paymaster wouldn't notice any one face more than he ought to. Marian and Murtaugh were cruising in one car; Sergeant Buchanan and one of his detectives in another. Both cars were equipped with radio receivers tuned to the frequency used by the mikes the detectives were wearing.

"Where's Captain DiFalco?" Murtaugh asked. "I'd have thought he wouldn't want to miss this."

"Gloria Sanchez says she left a note on his desk," Marian replied. "Right under the big stack of papers she found there."

Murtaugh looked away and smiled.

Marian ran a radio check. Someone in the Guggenheim might wonder at so many visitors wearing earplugs, but the courier wouldn't be there long enough to spot anything. The radio communication checked out, so long as Marian didn't drive too far from the corner of Fifth Avenue and Eighty-eighth Street.

Three o'clock.

A radio voice spoke. "Woman approaching Schumacher. Forty, kinda dumpy, shoulder-length brown hair. Tan all-weather coat and black boots."

Silence.

"She's the one. She just handed Schumacher the envelope. Now she's going out."

Another voice: "I got her." A pause of two minutes. "She's going into the park."

Gloria Sanchez: "I'm on her."

A longer pause.

"Guy sittin' on a bench in Central Park in February. Our paymaster?" Gloria paused a moment. "Yep, that's him. Just gave the courier an envelope. Dark hair, sallow complexion, wearin' just about the ugliest coat I've ever seen. Mustard-colored. Dirty mustard. The guy's nothin' to remember, but that coat's gonna stand out in a crowd."

Another minute passed.

"Just got a closer look at that coat. 'S well-cut, material's good—he musta paid plenty for it. Mebbe the guy's color-blind."

Marian clicked on her transmitter. "Gloria, you're talking too much."

"Yas'm." Two minutes later: "I'm droppin' off."

"I got him," a new voice said.

They followed the man in the mustard coat as he paid off another courier, in front of a Times Square camera shop—a second death ordered for that day. The paymaster next led them to an ordinary-looking office building on the West Side.

"Roberts is riding up in the elevator with him," a voice said.

Then after what seemed like a hundred years, Roberts reported: "He went into a place called Twenty-first Century Consultants."

"That's it," Murtaugh said with satisfaction. "Let's go get 'em."

* 36 *

When the police burst into Twenty-first Century Consultants—weapons drawn, yelling "Freeze!"—all they found was one terrified paymaster and one even more terrified woman.

The one inner office was empty. "Dust," Detective Dowd announced. "Place isn't used."

"Where's Virgil?" Marian demanded of the woman.

"I don't know!" she replied tearfully.

"Who's Virgil?"

"I don't know that either! I've never seen him!"

Marian turned to the paymaster.

"Don't look at me," he said. "This is as close as I ever got to him."

"That's crap," Sergeant Buchanan said. "You gotta know who he is. You work for 'im!"

"A lotta people work for 'im! You know why I came here today? To tell *her* I wanted to meet this Virgil."

"That's true," the tearful woman confirmed.

The paymaster had decided to try bluffing his way out. All he did was pay people off. Nothing illegal in that, was there? He picked up the pay packets here and met some couriers at different places and paid them. He was hired by phone and he received his instructions by phone. And that's all there was to it.

So why this sudden urge to meet Virgil?

Nothing sudden about it. He'd been trying to meet his employer for a long time, but he was sure the other woman hadn't been passing his messages on.

What other woman?

The one that worked here before *her*. This one was sorta new.

What happened to the other woman?

He didn't know. She'd been here for as long as he'd been working for Virgil, but then one day she just disappeared. So he thought he'd try his luck with the new woman.

She just disappeared. "Rosalind Bowman," Marian said to Murtaugh.

The woman said her job was just to pass on the money to the various paymasters—yes, more than one. The money was delivered by messengers already sealed into the envelopes. Some were big, some were little. She never actually handled the money itself. All she did was distribute the envelopes and let Virgil know if something went wrong.

Let him know? How did she do that?

She sat down at the computer. "I don't know anything about these machines, but this is what I do." She turned on the computer, and they all watched a communications program load automatically. The dialing directory had no numbers listed, but Entry Number 1 showed seven small black blocks.

"The phone number's concealed," Perlmutter said. "She doesn't know who she's calling."

The woman nodded. "I just type the number 'one'—and when the screen says 'Connect,' I type in my message. That's all."

Detective O'Toole said, "What if we type in that number 'one' right now?"

"It won't tell us anything," Perlmutter said. "But it will tell Virgil we've found this place, if she doesn't leave a message for him."

"So," the paymaster said, "you gonna let us go, or what? I didn't do anything."

Marian said, "Walker, Dowd—take them in and book them. Accessory to murder."

The paymaster started squawking and the woman started crying; but Walker and Dowd paid no attention and unceremoniously hauled them out. The place quieted down considerably once they'd gone.

Gloria Sanchez sat yoga-fashion on the desk. "So the paymaster was a lot smaller fry than we thought."

"Yes, we were naive there," Captain Murtaugh said, "thinking the paymaster would lead us directly to Virgil. How many more layers does that bastard have between himself and here?"

Roberts pointed at the screen. "We could cut through them all if we could just get that phone number."

Perlmutter sat down at the computer. He tapped at the keyboard for a bit and announced, "That communications program with the hidden phone number is the only thing in this computer, other than the operating system. There's just nothing else on the hard disk."

Murtaugh asked, "Is there any way of bringing out that phone number?"

"Depends on the kind of security, I guess," Perlmutter said, "but I wouldn't know how to do it. I don't think the police computer department could do it either. This isn't the kind of work they do." He smiled ruefully. "I hate to say it, Captain, but the FBI is better set up to handle this than we are."

"What about an outside consultant?" Marian asked. "Do we have funds for that?"

Murtaugh's eyes flickered. "Go ahead." She picked up the phone and punched in a number.

When he answered, Marian said, "Holland, we need to borrow André Flood."

Perlmutter had simply disconnected the computer and picked it up, leaving the monitor and keyboard behind. "It's the easiest way," he said.

Marian sent everyone else home and then drove Murtaugh, Perlmutter, and the computer to Holland's agency. By then the workday was over, so only Holland and André Flood were still there. Marian explained what was needed, and André got to work.

Holland drew Marian aside. "Why did you ask for André and not for me?"

"You told me he was better than you. I believed you."

He glowered.

Perlmutter was awestruck by his surroundings. "This is a *great* office. Wow. The private-eye business sure has changed."

Murtaugh asked, "You specialize in computer investigations, don't you, Holland? Security breaches, wire fraud, that sort of thing?"

"Primarily," Holland answered. "But not all investigations can be completed on the computer. We have to complement with good old plain detective work now and then."

Marian went into André's office and pulled up a chair next to the young man. "Would it distract you to tell me what you're doing?"

"Not at all," he said easily. "I'm simply running some preliminary programs looking for a back door into their security. I need to get inside before I can start searching for your phone number."

"Perlmutter said there was nothing on the disk except the communications program."

"Oh, it's hidden. It won't show up on any directory listing. But it's there." Suddenly, he turned to face Marian. "Thank you, Lieutenant."

"What for?"

"For bringing me this."

She smiled. "You really love it, don't you?"

He turned back to the screen. "It's the best of everything."

She was still trying to figure out an answer to that when Holland came in. He said something to André in what sounded to Marian like a foreign language. André answered in the same unintelligible speech. After a few minutes of that, Marian gave her chair to Holland and went back to the reception area.

Perlmutter was playing a game on the receptionist's computer. Murtaugh said, "Holland told me there'd be no charge for André's services."

"Oh. Good."

He gave her a small smile. "Is that going make a problem for you? Knowing we got this service free because you and he, er . . ."

"Oh, he's not doing it for me," Marian said. "He's doing it for you."

"For *me*?" He was astonished.

How to explain? "Captain, Holland has his own ways of doing things. He'll never say to you, 'I apologize for being rude.' What he'll say is, 'There's no charge for the service.'"

Murtaugh gave a half grunt, half laugh. "Are you sure?"

She wasn't. "I'm sure."

Holland came in to announce that André had found his back door. "Now the real work begins. It could take minutes, but it's more likely to take hours. If you want to go get something to eat—"

"We'll stay," Murtaugh decided for all of them.

An hour later Perlmutter was showing Marian how to play a computer game, while Murtaugh had found something to read. A chime sounded, making them all jump.

Holland came out of André's office and looked at the hall monitor. "It's Gloria Sanchez." He let her in.

"Hey, Holland." Gloria went straight to Marian. "I'm sorry, Marian—there shouldn't have been a delay. But the guys just didn't realize what it meant."

"What what meant?"

"The four men guarding Schumacher in the Guggenheim—they're all from the Ninth, they don't know the faces. That envelope the courier brought Schumacher. For his next hit?" She fished it out of her shoulder bag. "I think you'd better take a look."

Marian opened the flap and slid out a printed data sheet and two photographs. The photos were of Austin Knowles.

"Oh boy," said Perlmutter.

"Who is he?" Holland asked.

Gloria told him.

Murtaugh shook his head. "Christ, these people are ruthless!"

"Do you want me to pick him up?" Gloria asked.

"Yes, and the sooner the better," Marian said, handing back the envelope. "Show him that. He'll come willingly enough. Perlmutter—go with her. Just make sure he's locked up where nobody can get at him. I'll be along when we finish here."

"Right," Gloria said. "Come on, Pearl."

"Perlmutter," he said. They left.

"So," Holland said, "protective custody or arrest?"

Murtaugh shrugged. "About half and half at this stage, I'd say." He looked at Marian. "You're sure he'll talk?"

"Wouldn't you, with a contract out on you? Austin was only an inch from talking already—his lawyer was trying to work out an immunity deal with the DA. That little envelope is all it's going to take to convince him. He'll talk."

An hour later, André had the phone number.

"Well done, André," Holland said. "That would have taken me at least fifteen minutes longer. Now to get a name to go with that number."

"That won't take long," André said, starting to type. "Phone company records are easy to—"

"Wait, André," Holland cautioned. He turned to the two cops watching the screen. "Captain and Lieutenant. Perhaps you'd care to go for a short stroll . . . say, ten minutes?"

"That won't be necessary," Marian said. "Just look up O.K. Toys in the phone directory."

They all three stared at her.

"Well, do you have a Manhattan directory or not?"

André looked it up. "She's right. That number and the number for O.K. Toys are the same."

Marian nodded. "Oliver Knowles was Virgil."

* 37 *

"I have to tell you first about my parents," Austin Knowles said, and paused.

They waited.

Long fingers running through thinning blond hair. "It's hard. It's hard for me to talk about them." He took a deep breath. "I told you we were from Texas?"

"Yes," said Marian.

"Back before I came along," Austin said, "Oliver and Myrna Knowles were starving. That is not an exaggeration. Dirt-poor white trash. Unskilled, except for Oliver's ability to fashion toys out of bits and scraps . . . but nobody wanted to buy them. They had nothing.

"They stole, when they could. A woman's purse, when she wasn't looking. A bicycle they could sell. Once, when they hadn't eaten for two days, in desperation they decided to break into a grocery store. They picked out a small store run by a widow with a small child. They lived over the store, but there was no man in the house. That made them feel safe, you see. They waited until the middle of the night and broke in.

"She caught them. She came down the stairs and turned on the lights and screamed she was calling the police. They jumped her. She fought back but it didn't do any good . . .

they killed her. They hadn't planned to kill her—they just meant to shut her up. But they hit too hard, and she died. They sat there on the floor of that two-bit grocery store staring at each other, stunned to a state of inaction.

"Then they saw a child of about three standing on the stairway. He'd seen the whole thing.

"Myrna said a child that young couldn't identify them . . . he wouldn't even remember what had happened in a few more years. Oliver said they couldn't take the chance. He said that even though the boy probably didn't understand what he'd seen, they couldn't leave a live witness behind. What if he remembered it later, all at once, when he was grown? This was murder they'd done there that night, and the police never stopped looking for murderers. Myrna regretfully admitted he might be right.

"But when they came down to it, they simply couldn't bring themselves to kill a three-year-old child. So, instead, they took me with them."

He fell silent, staring at his hands clenched together on the table.

"Where was this?" Marian asked quietly. "In what part of Texas?"

"In Austin." He laughed humorlessly. "That's right. They named me after the place they found me." With an effort, he sat up straight. "Please understand, I knew none of this until last month. When my mother—Myrna—knew she was dying, she told me the story. I have no memory of that night in the grocery store."

Marian nodded. "But that's where it started. In that accidental killing in the store."

"That's where it started," he agreed. "When they found out they'd gotten away with it, Oliver got a little bolder. He picked a warehouse with one nightwatchman and deliberately killed the man. With the only one likely to walk in on him safely out of the way, Oliver could take his time looting the place. This was in the days before surveillance cameras and the like."

"Then what happened?"

"Then it became a pattern. Myrna told me Oliver boasted to her that his real talent lay in 'taking out the other guy,' not in making toys. Then the day came when someone paid Oliver to commit a murder. When he brought it off without any suspicion being directed against either him or the man who hired him, he gave up his burglaries forever. From that day on, he was a hired killer."

"This was still in Texas?"

"Yes. And what memories I have of those days are of a warm, comfortable home with two loving parents. Oliver used to get down on the floor and play with me. If you'd asked me two months ago, I'd have said I had a happy, normal childhood."

"Then what?"

"Then Oliver decided he was ready for the big time and moved his family to New York. Myrna was a little vague about times, but I don't think he spent more than three years perfecting his skills in Texas." His voice was bitter. "I remember going to school for the first time shortly after we arrived in this new big city. So I must have been about six.

"Evidently Oliver found immediate and steady employment. A killer who never got caught was in high demand. And the more successful he became, the more Myrna began to pull away from him. She became more and more troubled by what he was doing . . . but I guess she felt a kind of loyalty to him there for a while because she did share in that first killing.

"Somewhere along the line Oliver started subcontracting

his 'jobs'—he had more work than he could handle. Pretty soon he had a stable of killers he could call on, and he was able to ease up a little and just arrange for murders, move into the administrative side of the killing business. He hit upon the idea of opening a toy company. He still liked playing around with toys, but a company would give him the physical facilities he needed to run his real business. Also, he hoped O.K. Toys would convince Myrna that he'd turned legit, but she saw through the ploy. Where the code-name Virgil came from, I have no idea, nor how long he used it." Another humorless laugh.

"All these years, what I thought was my father's business was in reality just a killer's hobby. Nothing else. A hobby."

Marian waited for him to go on. When he didn't, she prompted, "Then Oliver and Myrna separated?"

"Yes. Myrna simply couldn't stomach living with him any longer, knowing what he'd become. I didn't know that at the time, of course. I thought she was just being unreasonable. She'd tell me he was an evil man, and I should have nothing to do with him. Then I'd go over to his new place for a visit, and there'd be the same old Dad I'd always known. I thought she was acting crazy.

"I know better now," he said bitterly. "When she was lying in that hospital bed, telling me all this, I tried to comfort her by reminding her that Oliver was retired now. He wouldn't be causing any more deaths—it was over. But it wasn't over, she said. The business was still thriving. Oliver had been training Dave Unger for years to take over, and Elmore Zook would be steering him until he felt Unger could handle it alone. Unger's a bookkeeper, not an innovator. He still needed Zook. But when Oliver eventually died, I would inherit the majority of shares in the business—they were legitimate shares, registered as O.K. Toys shares but really shares in . . . Virgil, Incorporated, I suppose you could call it. Zook and Unger together are Virgil now, I guess.

"Myrna said those two would undoubtedly cheat me blind, but they'd keep me supplied with enough money to prevent my getting suspicious. But whatever money I got, it was going to be blood money. Do you realize I've lived over half my life supported by money paid for murder? That blood money sent me to college, paid for my architectural training, helped me open my own office? And blood money was to be my legacy. Myrna said she couldn't go to her grave leaving me in ignorance.

"The last time I saw Myrna—it was the day she died—I asked her who my real mother was. Myrna started to cry. That dying, guilt-ridden old woman, lying in a hospital bed and crying . . . because she couldn't remember my real mother's name."

Suddenly he looked up. "Could I have some water? I'm getting awfully dry."

Marian nodded to Austin's guard and waited until the bluesuit had returned with a paper cup of water. Austin swallowed it all down without taking a breath and then crumpled up the cup.

"After Myrna died," Marian said, "you decided something had to be done."

Austin nodded slowly. "I'd never really felt true hatred for another person before. But I hated Oliver. I hated him so much it was eating me alive. All those nice childhood memories—they were as phony as everything else about the man. I felt so cheated! Can you understand that? Everything about the first half of my life was a fraud!"

"So what did you do?"

"I wanted Oliver dead. It struck me as wonderfully ironic if he should be killed by the very organization he founded.

So I went to Elmore Zook and Dave Unger. I told them if they would arrange to have Oliver killed immediately, I'd turn all my shares in O.K. Toys over to them. They could have the whole thing." A sarcastic laugh. "Zook and Unger proved to be good friends to Oliver. They made me wait a whole day while they talked it over. *One day* it took them to decide to kill a man they'd been in business with for—well, in Zook's case, close to forty years. Oh yes—Oliver always knew how to find men exactly like himself."

Marian leaned forward on the table. "But it didn't work out the way you thought, did it, Austin? It didn't solve your problem. In fact, it just created a whole lot of new ones."

"Yes! That's what happened. Oliver's death didn't bring me the *relief* I thought it would. I realized I hadn't changed a thing. O.K. Toys would go on for years. People were still getting murdered for a fee. I got to thinking about how many people must be taking part in the venture to keep it going so well. Even if Dave Unger eased out all the legitimate toy people over the years, he still needed office staff— records people, computer people, his secretary. Did they know? Were they in for a cut? And what about Oliver's personal secretary? Surely Lucas Novak knew—how could his personal secretary *not* know? I even found myself looking at Mrs. R—Mrs. R, a housekeeper, for god's sake—and thinking that she'd lived under the same roof with Oliver for twenty years . . . she *had* to know what kind of man he was! I began to feel I was surrounded by people for whom murder for hire was no more extraordinary a way to earn a living than selling shoes. It was driving me crazy."

"And Zook and Unger saw it happening to you."

"Zook saw. I never know what Unger sees."

"What did Zook do?"

"Well, first he kept telling me to get a grip on myself.

Then he started saying I should go away for a while, take a vacation. Once he was so exasperated with me that he reminded me what kind of business O.K. Toys really is."

"A threat."

"I took it as such, yes."

"Then what happened?"

He smiled sadly. "Then you advised me to find a new lawyer." He played with the crumpled water cup a moment and then said, "I'd just had enough. That's all. It's an intolerable situation. All at once it simply became clear that that's what I should do. Find a new lawyer and admit my part in what's been going on. Maybe put a stop to this madness."

Marian said, "When you hired a new lawyer, Zook knew they'd lost you for good. So they went to their standard solution—they put out a contract on you. Unger made the necessary phone calls, and they thought their problem was solved."

He was shaking his head. "Solving problems—that's what this is all about, isn't it? If you have a tough problem, hire a man with a gun to take care of it for you." He noticed the look on her face. "Yes, I know, I did the same thing myself. But if I can help you put O.K. Toys out of business, maybe I can make up a little for what I did and for what my fa—what Oliver did, for all those years. Are you going to arrest Zook and Unger?"

"We arrested them both an hour ago," Marian said.

* 38 *

"So they're all three guilty," Murtaugh said.

"All three," Marian replied. "But Oliver Knowles was the guiltiest of them all."

"There's something missing in people like that. Some essential part's been left out."

"I got off the track there for a while, thinking Oliver was just a victim. I should have known Unger wasn't capable of thinking up a big scam all by himself."

"Well, that's when we were thinking the toy company was being set up for a new scam."

"True. And Virgil had been in business a long time. How long would you say . . . about forty years? That's how long Zook had been Oliver Knowles's lawyer."

"Sounds about right. My god. Forty years of killing people without getting caught."

"They must have rotated their shooters a lot. Killing was their profession, and they ran the business like professionals."

"Unfortunately. I wonder how many Virgils there are in this country."

"Well, Schumacher gave a list of some of them to *her*."

The "her" was Assistant District Attorney Julia Perry, who'd followed them out of the interrogation room. Right behind her was Austin Knowles's new lawyer, James Archer, silver-haired and silver-tongued.

Archer was patting at his perspiring forehead with a folded handkerchief. "This is going to make one interesting trial."

"In many ways," the prosecutor agreed.

"I think we've got extreme provocation here."

"Oh, I don't know," Perry said. "Austin is more Oliver's son than he knows. They both reacted to stress in the same way—by killing."

Archer snorted. "That'll never fly."

She smiled. "Wanna bet?"

The two attorneys said good night and left.

The captain and his lieutenant headed back toward their offices. Marian said, "There was some chink in Virgil's defenses that we missed."

"Oh?"

"Rosalind Bowman—when she was working in that office of Virgil's . . . Twenty-first Century Consultants? When she was there, she must have stumbled across something that made her suspect Oliver Knowles. She wouldn't have had him followed otherwise. She had no other connection with Knowles."

"Too bad we can't ask her."

"Yes, the lady's long gone." Marian wished her well. "We still don't know why Unger opened a new Swiss account and then closed it again."

"Maybe he didn't. We didn't check on it, did we? Maybe that secretary who told Perlmutter about the account simply saw the handwriting on the wall and was trying to play Little Miss Innocent for the police."

She looked at him. "God. I never even thought of that."

"Well, it'll all come out in the wash. I'm more interested in finding out how Virgil's clients got in touch with the organization in the first place. I wonder how we can get Unger to talk."

"Tell him Zook said to."

Murtaugh smiled. "That may be what it'll take." They came to Marian's office first; he waited while she got her coat and bag. "So what happens next?"

"So next we turn André Flood loose on the O.K. Toys computers. Once he uncovers those hidden files, we're going to be so busy making arrests we won't have time for anything else." They walked on to his office. "I want to get every one of them. Every person in this city who bought a death. I don't want even one to slip through our fingers. Not even the one tonight."

Murtaugh put on his coat, wrapped a muffler around his throat. "What one tonight?"

They started down the stairs. "The courier who delivered the envelope to Schumacher—she wasn't the only one the paymaster met," Marian said. "He paid off a second courier after that, remember? In Times Square." She hated the thought of it. "Somebody died tonight—because of Virgil."

"Larch." He stopped at the foot of the stairs, forcing her to stop too. "Whoever that person was who died tonight—that was Virgil's last victim. It's over. Finished. You put an end to it yourself. This is a cause for rejoicing."

"I know. I'm just tired."

He sighed. "Lord, so am I. I'm going to spend the entire weekend sleeping. Good night, Larch. See you on Monday."

"Night, Captain."

It was almost four A.M. when she started her car to go home. But she didn't want to go home; she didn't want to go there at all. She headed the car toward Central Park West. When she'd parked and ridden up to his floor, she let herself in with the key he'd sent her.

He was still awake. "Is it finished?" he asked quietly.

"Yes. It's finished."

"And you? Are you all right?"

"Yes. As if I've been rubbed raw—but all right."

"It's an abrasive business you're in. It can coarsen you and cheapen you, if you let it."

"Prevention can be difficult."

"But not impossible. Don't give all of yourself. Keep some part of yourself separate, private."

"I will . . . consider it."

He moved over to her and gently removed her coat. "I'm glad you're home," he said.

About the Author

Barbara Paul's novels for Scribner include *The Apostrophe Thief*, *You Have the Right to Remain Silent*, *In-laws and Outlaws*, *He Huffed and He Puffed*, *But He Was Already Dead When I Got There*, and *The Renewable Virgin*. Ms Paul, who is working on a new Marian Larch novel, lives in Pittsburgh.